Trepan Skylights
or
Enlightenment the Hard Way

Dog & Vile short fiction

First published 2023
'Three Coats of Paint' © Mark Keane
'Matt in my House' © Rebecca Dearden
'Just a Day Off' © Hana Morska
'In Hawaii on Mars' © Ben Duncan
'Swabland' © Gadzooks Marchmain
'Gore' © Andrew Hart
'Psychoneuroses' © Evan Hay
'Brickwork' © Robert Graham
'Victims' © David Rogers
'The Electric Jesus Vagina' © Steve Carter
ISBN: 9798869961488
dogandvile@gmail.com
Cover art © Ray Bass
'Just a Day Off' first published in
T'Art, Literature and Visual Arts Magazine

Dog and Vile

CONTENTS

I'm sorry, I don't remember your name, but I found that email address you wrote on the frontispiece of my *Wind in the Willows* first edition. Thank you for asking me to contribute a foreword to your collection thingy. 'Enlightenment the hard way', I think you said. So … what comes to mind is an incident that occurred six years ago, while I was supervising my rescue badgers as they gambolled outside my Vale of Health maisonette. I heard raised voices and walked down the garden to see an argument between some adolescents who looked like they might live in Enfield. Shuttling in cerebration between social totality and the irreducible complexity of individual need, I hoped for a peaceful resolution, but a nasty free-for-all broke out. Throwing caution to the winds, I intervened in an effort to shield my babies, crying out that violence did no one any credit. At some point in the mêlée, a craft blade was stabbed into my thyroid and I lost consciousness. Buffy Pethwick at twenty-three told me that the lads hoisted me shoulder-high and sang lustily as they carried me around my garden, before throwing me through my kitchen window. I then underwent five blood transfusions and spent the next three years relearning how to speak, move and toilet unassisted. I found this experience enlightening, and now tend to mind my own business. Is this the kind of thing you had in mind?

I repeated the words 'Quebec snow' like a mantra, squeezed my hands, broken fingernails biting into the soft flesh, and willed myself to believe

Three Coats of Paint | Mark Keane

Tony France came looking for me in the garden maze where I was pruning the hedges.

'You can leave that for now,' he said. 'Mr Davidson has a special job for you.'

'What's he got in mind?' I asked.

'I'll let him explain.'

I followed Tony into the house and up the marble stair-case.

We waited on the second-floor landing for Mr Davidson to join us. He led the way into a room with floor-to-ceiling shelves packed with books. Tiffany lamps in each corner cast diffuse light. The bocote wood floor was burnished to a rich brown sheen.

In front of one set of shelves stood a four-sided struc-ture with a zig-zag arrangement, like an expanded con-certina. Four grey plastered surfaces, nine-feet high and fifteen-feet wide, each with a six-inch wooden skirting board. Three plastic tubs stacked to one side of the structure bore labels that read: brilliant white.

Mr Davidson pointed to the tubs. 'You have been provided with six gallons of paint. Three coats will be required.' He adjusted the cuffs of his bespoke suit. 'I want the final effect to capture the whiteness I witnessed following a heavy snowfall in Quebec in January 1981. You will receive credit for any paint you do not use. That credit is, of course, predicated on your achieving the requisite whiteness of the Quebec snow.'

He paused, hands clasped behind his back. 'On no account are you to get any paint on the wooden border or on the floor. No dripping is permitted. You will not be given any cloth or tissue. If you attempt to cover up mistakes, there will be grave consequences.' He pursed his lips. 'Joe Spain certainly regrets his carelessness.'

Muffled buzzing came from Mr Davidson's pocket. He took out his phone and checked the screen.

'I have a meeting to attend. Tony can cover the logistics.'

He exited the room, every inch the autocrat.

I waited until he was definitely gone.

'What did he mean about Joe Spain?'

'Joe Spain won't be painting anything for some time.' Tony nodded his head slowly, eyebrows raised, making it clear he had nothing more to say on the subject.

One thing had struck me as odd since signing on with Mr Davidson—all his employees had countries for surnames: Tony France, Ivan Israel, Hugh Peru and now Joe Spain.

'What's the reason for the painting?' I asked. 'What was all that stuff about Quebec snow?'

'Don't ask me. I just work for the man.'

'Is it a test?'

'Who knows?' Tony puffed out his cheeks. 'If it is, you'd better pass it.'

Up close, the four surfaces were not smooth but covered in dimples and ridges, edges and corners.

'How am I to know if I've got the right colour?'

Tony shrugged. 'Use your imagination. The boss suggested three coats of paint, and he should know.' He glanced at his watch. 'Time to lock you in for the night.'

He showed me a small adjoining room where I was to sleep. It contained a cot with a hessian cover, a wooden chair and a chamber pot. There was no bulb hanging from the ceiling, no lamp.

'Someone will be back at eight in the morning with your breakfast. Probably me or Ivan. Get a good night's sleep, you've a lot of painting ahead of you. One coat per day. Not as easy as you might think. Heavy work. Not physically, but mentally. Mr Davidson will be here on Friday to check the final result.' He leaned a little closer. 'I remember Joe Spain's first night. He was cocksure. Painting a wall was a piece of piss, I remember him saying. He's not saying that now.'

Tony locked the door. His footsteps faded, and an eerie stillness pervaded the enclosed space, inky black apart from a grey line where a gap under the door seeped pale light from the outer room. I lay on the cot and didn't sleep.

The following morning, Ivan unlocked the door. I sat up, and checked my watch—it was coming up to ten o'clock.

'I know I'm late, Taffy.' Ivan put a tray on the ground. 'Better dig in. You've got to finish the first coat by five o'clock. Mr Davidson's instructions.'

I hadn't had much to do with Ivan Israel, and found him

off-hand to the point of hostility. Tall and paunchy with a precarious comb-over and perpetual sneer, he always gave the impression I'd wronged him in some way.

I needed no encouragement to dig in. A top notch breakfast, but I expected nothing less from Mr Davidson. Blueberry porridge, crispy bacon with waffles and maple syrup, eggs benedict, freshly squeezed orange juice and a carafe of Columbian roast.

Ivan reappeared in the doorway. 'This is a one-brush job,' he announced.

He handed me the brush, large and unwieldy with thick bristles. I turned it in my hand and could see it had been used before. There were white stains on the handle and dried paint at the base of the bristles.

'Is this what—'

'Same brush Joe Spain used.' Ivan cut me off. 'I hope you do a better job than him.'

I thought about the wooden border, and Mr Davidson's warning about mistakes. 'Do you have a second?'

'One-brush job. Mr Davidson's instructions. You better crack on, Taffy. No time to waste.' Ivan turned away and called over his shoulder, 'Someone will bring you lunch at one o'clock.'

I stood in front of the structure. The dimples and depressions I'd noticed the day before didn't appear to be part of a design. A series of intricate rucks reminded me of the backbone of an animal. The light from the lamps threw complex shadows that caused the undulations and hollows to shift position. Hardly the best light for painting. Mr Davidson was testing me and, as Tony said, I'd better pass the test.

10

I lifted the top tub, my arms wobbling with the effort, and lugged it over to the structure. Ivan had provided no tools other than the brush, nothing to lever the lid from the tub. A hard plastic sheath ran around the rim, which had to be removed before the lid could be released. I pulled and twisted, cut my fingers on the hard plastic, and finally ripped it from the tub. Using the key to my flat, I pried open the lid bit by bit, until it popped up.

My fingers throbbed, nails broken, cuts stinging. I tore the hem of my shirt, and wrapped the cloth around the cuts. The paint was thick and yellowish—anything but brilliant white. I tried using the brush handle to stir it but that made no difference. Five hours to go and I still hadn't applied a single drop of paint.

By the time Hugh Peru showed up, I had covered the upper half of one surface. To reach the top, I stood on the chair from my room. Getting up and down from the chair, I worried about dripping paint on the floor and cupped my hand under the brush. The paint missed out depressions in the surface. I poked the white tip of the bristles into the hollows. The brush wasn't up to the job, the lighting inadequate and misleading.

'Something smells good.' Hugh held up a dome-covered platter. 'Better eat while it's still hot.'

Unlike Ivan Israel, Hugh Peru was invariably cheery. A small man in his mid-thirties with curly black hair and an enormous moustache, he could have stepped out of a Velásquez painting.

He handed me the platter and moved to one side to examine the wall. 'You've made real progress.'

11

'It's hopeless,' I said. 'The paint isn't going on properly.'

Hugh shook his head. 'The first coat always looks like that. You're too much of a perfectionist. I'll leave you to eat in peace. Bon appétit.'

I lifted the dome, and the warm waft of flavours got my digestive juices flowing. Venison steak in a red wine sauce, garlic mash and white asparagus tips. A glass of burgundy to wash it down, and cheesecake for afters. Unlike paint brushes, Mr Davidson didn't skimp when it came to food. I refused to linger over the meal; no time for such luxury. When Hugh returned, I had resumed painting.

'How was lunch?'

'Very tasty.' I held out the brush. 'How am I supposed to avoid getting paint on the wood with this?'

'I see.' Hugh grimaced. 'Very difficult. I suppose you need to be extra careful. We don't want a repeat of the Joe Spain incident.'

'There must be a second brush I can use—a smaller one to do along the border.'

'Afraid not. Instructions from Mr Davidson. A one-brush job, that's what he said. You'll work it out.' He patted my shoulder. 'Better get a move on. You have to be finished by five. Ivan will be here to shut up shop.' He dawdled in the doorway. 'You'll get it done. I've every confidence in you. You're nothing like Joe Spain.'

I picked up the pace, moving down the first surface to within three inches of the wooden border. Any closer and I risked getting paint on the wood. I needed a smaller brush. Using my key, I hacked off enough bristles to fashion a precision brush. I should have kept the knife from lunch; it would have come in handy to cut the bristles, and to open the other tubs. No doubt Mr Davidson wouldn't have permitted it, as part of his instructions.

I removed a shoelace and tied it around the bristles to bind them together. Then, I got down on my knees, and applied paint with this bristle brush. Slowly, painstakingly, I moved the bristles from left to right, covering the area above the wooden strip. It worked. Starting at an angle of forty-five degrees, the tip just above the border, I let the paint grip and then drew the bristles away from the wooden edge. I followed this with a horizontal alignment, and a smooth motion to the right. Inching along, knees bruised by the hard ground, my breathing synchronised with my hand movements. Nothing existed but the wooden strip. I kept going, all the way to the end of the fourth surface.

I eased myself off the ground. Ten minutes to four, and I had the better part of three surfaces to complete. I attacked the paint, shoved the big brush into the tub, pulled it out, paused and painted up-stroke, down-stroke, to the right, up and down, a check to fill dimples, pressing the tip into corners, another press and twist. Back into the tub, careful not to drip paint. I persevered: mechanical, indefatigable; a painting machine. When the tub was light enough to lift, I carried it with me, minimising the chances of spillage and allowing much quicker work. I brushed, and dipped, and probed, and squeezed, until I completed the final section.

Ivan arrived at five o'clock. I hid the makeshift bristle brush in my pocket.

He walked from one end of the structure to the other. 'Looks like you got it finished after all, Taffy. Very messy though.' He hunkered down and inspected the border. 'Better hope you don't slip-up. Mr Davidson will be here on Friday with special lamps to check for mistakes.'

I said nothing, too exhausted to speak or think. Ivan checked the tub of paint.

'There's still a lot left; you might have stinted on the paint. Right, put the lid back on and I can lock up.' He picked up the brush. 'What were you doing, Taffy? Painting or scrubbing the walls? I'll have this cleaned so it's ready for you in the morning.'

He locked the door behind me. I lay on the cot, curled into a ball and fell asleep.

Tony France brought breakfast at nine o'clock. Not as lavish as the morning before—two slices of buttered toast, a Danish pastry and a cup of tea.

'Ready for the second coat?' he asked.

'I suppose so.'

He waited in the outer room. When I finished breakfast, he handed me the brush, the bristles stiff and the handle white with paint.

'Word of advice: use more paint on the second coat.' He took away the plate and cup. 'Same arrangement as yesterday. Finish by five. Ivan or Hugh will bring you lunch.'

I took the bristle brush from my pocket. It was unusable, hard and unpliable from dried paint. No matter; I felt calm and assured, now that I had my technique. I used my key to saw off more bristles. In no rush, I sat on the first tub, breathed deeply and pictured smooth white surfaces. I dipped the big brush into the paint, instinctively gauging the correct depth and load. In less than half an hour I had painted the top half of one surface.

Onto the bottom half, no hesitation or uncertainty, in total command of the task. I reached the border and stopped for a short break to prepare myself for the next stage. I grasped the bristle brush—it felt natural, an extension of my hand. Angled strokes preceded horizontal strokes, in fluid motion, to complete the first side. I scraped the paint from the bottom of the tub for touch-ups. This time, I had no difficulty removing the plastic sheath and opening the second tub. I continued along the border, angled and horizontal brushstrokes, repetitive and relentless.

I didn't hear Hugh enter the room.

'You're going great guns,' he said.

He watched as I finished one more border section. I made no attempt to hide the bristle bush, and left it lying on the lid. Hugh nodded his head appreciatively.

'You've really got the hang of it.'

He carried a smaller dish with no cover: a bowl of oxtail soup for starters, two sausages and one potato for the main course, a glass of soda water, but no dessert. I ate the food quickly. Hugh kept up a lively chatter but I didn't listen. I wanted him gone so I could get back to work.

He went into the small room and returned with the chamber pot.

'I'll empty this for you.'

I sipped the soda water and planned my strategy—finish the borders first, and then return to the top.

Hugh returned, chamber pot held aloft. 'You're good to go.' He collected the dish and glass. 'I'll leave you to it. Remember to finish by five.'

The final stages with the bristle brush completed, I returned to the mother brush. A fluent sequence of strokes, up and down, in an elegant flow; an elegance, too, in the precise incursions into corners and depressions. I kept at it, oblivious to the surroundings or purpose of what I was doing. The task required my full attention; the physical act of painting was purpose enough.

I had finished and sealed the second tub when Ivan appeared. Seeing his snide expression, I put the bristle brush in my pocket, not wanting any trouble.

'No time to waste, Taffy. I've things to do.' He lifted the empty tub. 'Have you finished with this?' He surveyed the structure and grimaced. 'You better hope the third coat works. That doesn't look like the colour of any snow I've ever seen.'

He ushered me into my room, and locked the door. I sat on the cot and brooded over what he'd said. There was no denying the surfaces had looked streaky—the third coat would have to be decisive.

Hugh Peru unlocked the door the next morning. I was already up and pacing the available space.

'The day of the third coat; a most auspicious day.' Hugh held the door open and waved me through. 'Breakfast is served.'

He handed me a glass of water and a plate with a slice of bread. The brush lay on one of the remaining tubs, looking the worse for wear, bristles separated and handle thick with paint.

Hugh gestured to the wall. 'It's looking good. I feel cold just thinking about that Quebec snow.'

16

I chewed the bread, which was hard at the edges, and drank the water. Hugh leaned against the bookshelves and checked his phone. I passed him the plate and empty glass.

'Ivan will be here with lunch. Keep up the good work.' He gave me a thumbs-up. 'Mr Davidson is bound to be pleased.'

My eyes ached after a night of fitful sleep. The walls appeared greyer and streakier than I'd anticipated. I returned to my room to get the chair, and sat facing the structure. A final concerted effort, I just had to ignore my weariness and the hollowness in my stomach. I repeated the words 'Quebec snow' like a mantra, squeezed my hands, broken fingernails biting into the soft flesh, and willed myself to believe.

Seven hours left. Precious hours and minutes and seconds. Urgency fizzing in my veins, I pried open the lid and entered the snowstorm, up and down the chair, paint from brush to wall. Paint and snow. Back and forth, more and more paint—every depression and edge, ridge and dimple, under thick, fluffy Quebec snow.

I cut off the optimum number of bristles, and began along the border. Bristle brush at an angle and then horizontal, moving higher, encroaching the upper third coat. Then the mother brush to smooth the overlap and achieve the oneness of brilliant snowy white. One surface finished, then onto the next, and into the third tub. I bent down, legs straddling the tub, bristle brush into the paint and onto the wall, switching to mother brush, tub and wall.

A quarter of the way across, my rumbling stomach caused me to hesitate and I missed the switch of brushes, using the mother brush on the border. A splodge of paint stuck to the wood, glaringly white.

I shuffled backwards, shocked and outraged. After two days, and more than four gallons of paint—how could this happen? Walking in circles, I groaned and cursed the brush and wanted to lie down and sleep. No way. No giving up; not when I'd come this far. Giving up was not an option.

I tore a strip from my shirt and used it to sponge the misapplied paint, spreading and smudging the stain. I spat on the cloth, rubbed and rubbed until the paint had gone. No evidence of the mistake remained, not to my eyes at least. But would Mr Davidson know? I pressed on, slower now, ultra-careful. I could allow one mistake, but no more than one.

Ivan carried in a tray with another slice of bread and a glass of water.

He gave me one of his derisive grins. 'So, Taffy, what've you been up to?'

I said nothing. His grin broadened as though he read my mind.

'Any slip-ups? If you ask me the whole thing looks botched. Mr Davidson isn't going to accept this. Snowy landscape? More like badly mixed concrete.'

He nudged the tray with the toe of his shoe. 'Have your bread and water so I can get going.'

I chewed the stale bread, keeping my eyes away from the spot where I'd splodged paint. Ivan scanned the books on the shelves and hummed something that sounded like a nursery rhyme. I considered asking him what he honestly thought of the painting but decided against it.

He took the plate and glass. 'Finish everything by five. Good luck, Taffy. You're going to need it.'

I returned to the border, on my knees, hypersensitive and vigilant. All that mattered was the brushstroke, then the next stroke, bristle brush and mother brush. I completed the border; no visible overlap, a continuum of white. One more check on the area where I'd slipped up—I couldn't see anything but wood grain. How could Mr Davidson tell? His eyesight was no better than mine. He would never know, and I had no intention of telling him.

Entering the home stretch, I painted with renewed vigour. The third tub was severely depleted but enough remained to finish the job. I applied the paint thickly. It went on like a dream, the whiteness lighting the room. I scrutinised the surfaces, searching for paler areas, my tired eyes straining to find blemishes. Absorbed in this search, I didn't notice Tony France until he stood beside me.

'Job done,' he said.

I secured the lid on the tub, pressing down so it snapped shut. As I handed over the brush, I experienced a surge of sadness—the painting ended, there was nothing left to do, or worth doing.

'Do you think Mr Davidson will like it?'

Tony took a step back, as if recoiling from my question. 'That's not for me to say. All I can say is that you've done a better job than Joe Spain.'

Emboldened, I asked, 'What exactly did Joe Spain do wrong?'

Tony took his time before answering. 'It was more his attitude. Joe had a poor attitude. He didn't show the work enough respect. We can't say that about you.'

I went into my room. Tony stood in the doorway.

'I'll be here in the morning with Mr Davidson for the final verdict.'

When he left, I sat on the cot, got up and stood in the darkness, and sat down again. Sleep seemed unimportant as I vacillated between hope and disquiet. I pictured whiteness emanating from the surfaces in the other room. Then I recalled Mr Davidson's reference to grave consequences, and Tony saying that Joe Spain wouldn't be painting anything for some time. And, of course, there were those special lights Mr Davidson would use to check for mistakes.

I slipped into semi-consciousness. The sound of a key in the lock woke me. Tony opened the door.

'Mr Davidson will be joining us shortly. Come on out and wait.'

We stood by the painted structure. I stared at the ground, afraid to look up, and possibly see the area where I'd splodged paint, or the inadequacy of the whiteness.

Mr Davidson arrived, dapper as ever. His eyes widened when he saw me, and I realised how I must appear—exhausted, bearded and gaunt from hunger. And my clothes, torn and covered in paint, thick smears on my sleeves and across my trousers.

He stood with his hands on his hips and rocked back and forth. 'Well, Oscar. I can call you Oscar, can't I?'

'Yes,' I replied.

'Oscar Wales is quite a mouthful.' He smiled, the merest uplift of his lips. 'Well, Oscar, you've been busy.'

I waited for his verdict, but Mr Davidson appeared to be in no hurry. He wasn't even looking at the structure. Where were the special lights? Was the painting good enough? Did it remind him of the snow that fell in Quebec in January 1981?

'Well, Oscar.' He turned towards the concertina surfaces, his face impassive.

I looked. The structure appeared white, brilliant white, but was it what he wanted? The leadenness in my stomach told me it wasn't.

He began walking towards the door. Tony indicated that I should follow him.

'Oscar, I have an interesting project for you.' Mr Davidson paused, and coughed to clear his throat. 'It relates to a visit I made in 1987 to a small village in the Urals. An area surrounded by forest, magnificent old oaks. Late September: the colour of the leaves was quite magnificent. Something I will never forget.' He looked over his shoulder. 'Tony, please take us to the other room.'

With Tony in front, I accompanied Mr Davidson, down a long hallway with thick-piled wool carpeting. Relieved and excited, I could barely take in what he was saying.

'You will be provided with six gallons of paint. The effect I want you to capture is the colour and texture of those leaves that I witnessed in that village in the Urals in September 1987. Three coats of paint will be required.'

Tony stopped at a door and took a set of keys from his pocket. My neck tingled. I flexed my fingers and slowed my breathing, joyful and anxious. Another challenge.

His car is black and flat to the ground, like it's been driven over by a steamroller. He's parked in next-door's spot but, thankfully, they're away. I wouldn't have wanted to rush down and my first words be 'would you mind moving your car?'

Matt at my House | Rebecca Dearden

Either my friend Chris is a big fan of Matt Damon, or I got an actual text from Matt. The text said: 'Want to see Jason Bourne tonight? Love Matt Damon. X.'

Let's look on the bright side. It's from Matt.

'Hi Matt. Nice to hear from you. Lee's at work all day tomorrow. Do you fancy coming up for a while? Could you make sure you're not followed? Oh, and bring some oat milk and some guns. Love, R x.'

'Hello Rachel. I'll see you tomorrow. Only problem is, all my shirts are dirty so I will have to arrive shirtless. I'll carry the gun in a holster along with a few oatcakes. Funny this, really. No one ever says, "Hey, Matt Damon, fancy baking a cake?" You know what? Sometimes I do like baking. I like guns more, though.'

It's tomorrow now and I've just realised he doesn't know my address. It's only a fleeting anxiety. I can feel the satellite's eye zooming in through the trees that look like broccoli from above. And there I am, in a clearing, dressed in red, waving upwards from my patio.

I don't think we'll have sex today, so I don't need to work out how to tell him I only have one breast. That can happen later when he's already too much in love to care.

Perhaps I should have been more specific. Does 'bring some guns' say enough? I haven't invited Mr Ripley or a Martian, for goodness sake. I think it's clear, and he did say he'd come without a shirt. He knows what's expected. He's used to being directed.

Here he comes now. I can see a dust cloud and there are tyres screeching around the hairpin bend. He'll appreciate that bend, although it's a natural feature, of course. I can't take credit, though maybe I shouldn't be so modest. I did choose to live here.

Great. His car is black and almost flat to the ground, like it's been driven over by a steamroller. He's parked in next-door's spot but, thankfully, they're away. I wouldn't have wanted to rush down and my first words be 'would you mind moving your car?' He's not getting out straightaway; perhaps just taking a quick call or sending a text message. He might drive very fast and sometimes knock other cars out of the way but he'd never use the phone while driving. I can hear him saying 'you don't survive torture and knife fights only to hit a lamppost while looking at Facebook'. He's got a nice shy smile when he says that.

Oh, he looks very pleasant indeed. Quite immediately American, somehow. He does have a shirt on after all, which I'm rather glad about, because I wouldn't feel right looking at a bare chest, plus I haven't lit the fire. He's coming up the steps two at a time and he's brought flowers. He's also holding a Co-op bag, so that's probably the fake milk. I wonder if he misunderstood about Oatly milk and thought I meant oatcakes?

I hope he doesn't walk around too much when he's in the house. His walk is unparalleled. He might pace around telling me something important, but I wouldn't be able to listen. I'd just watch the walk and marvel. However, I do think I might ask him to do his Matthew McConaughey impression, which would be a good ice-breaker, although it would definitely involve his taking off his shirt. Something for a bit later in the evening.

He's here at the open patio doors. I'll speak first to show it's just a normal day for me and he's got no need to feel awkward. I'm a real person, no airs or graces, and he'll be able to relax and talk freely to me.

'Hello Matt. It's very nice to meet you.'

'You too, Rachel. I hope you're not feeling awkward at all? Don't be overawed by my being a film star. I'm a real person underneath it all, you know. No airs and graces. It'll be relaxing to spend a day just being myself with someone I can talk freely to. I really could do with a cuppa—isn't that what you say here?'

How lovely that he's bothered to learn my language. While I'm putting on the kettle and explaining the types of tea he could choose, or coffee, if he prefers, he's doing a quick sweep of the room for bugs. He looks a bit suspicious of the squirrel knocking on the window for its usual walnut. Surveillance drones these days—they come in all shapes and sizes and you can't be too careful. I'd recognise that particular squirrel anywhere, though, and Matt's reassured. His gun is well hidden, which is such a thoughtful gesture.

When we're sitting down with our drinks, Matt asks me to tell him all about myself—who's in my family and what sort of life I have. I haven't been talking long when Matt's attention seems to wander, or rather he looks suddenly more attentive, but not towards me. I feel a little hurt for a second until I hear the slight engine noise too. He's quite different when he's so alert, like a sort of vibrating rock. I reach out to touch his shoulder, just to see if it's as hard as it looks, but then he's instantly standing.

It's all very fast now. Matt says nothing but his eyes are darting around. I have to make sure I'm right in front of him and staring hard to see what his eyes are doing—a quick glance at his car, which I think means he knows he's been found; a turn of the head to the front door, then the patio door; a sideways glance at the Wi-Fi box and the waving Chinese cat. Then he's up and we're both out.

He's pushing me in front of him and we're running up the steps in the garden. At the top, he throws me, and then himself, down onto the ground behind the big rock and manages somehow to also cover my red T-shirt with some bracken. The engine noise is louder, but it's nice and comfortable here in the grass and I could probably fall asleep if Matt's breathing wasn't quite so exciting.

Seconds later, a helicopter rises up in a perfectly straight vertical from the valley and hovers in front of the neighbours' house. There's an almighty din, like chainsaws being thrown at a cliff-face, and their verandah is now hanging off.

I've probably raised my head above the crocosmia a bit too much, because Matt squashes my face back down into the grass. I can still see out of one eye that the helicopter has done what it wanted to do and is turning round to leave. I start to get up, but Matt is up first and halfway down the banking. He signals for me to stay where I am. This new sitting area Lee built is a fantastic vantage point. It doesn't get as much sun as I'd hoped, but there's a lovely view of the moors and next-door's garden.

Matt, however, has disappeared. Not for long, though—there's a crash of breaking glass and next-door's kitchen window is all over the path. Something wriggling inside a rolled-up curtain is thrown out, disentangles itself and there's the neighbour's dog bolting for the woods, followed by the cat.

Matt comes out of the window headfirst, like he's diving, somersaults on the lawn and is back on his feet. I clap and clap, until I see he's looking at the sky in the distance. Here comes the helicopter again. He's got only seconds to get off the grass, back up the slope and to drag me over the wall into the field before something comes out of the front of the helicopter. Most of next-door seems to lift into the air, explode and then fall back down in pieces.

The helicopter turns again and Matt's off back down the slope. There's not really a door any more, but he runs in between the stone uprights that are just about still standing and vanishes into the dust and rubble. There are flames all over, but I'm not worried. You just wouldn't be, would you? Look at what he's coped with in the past, you'd think.

Well, immediately, I am worried because there he is falling out of the front of the house, just where the bay window used to be. I can't see his face, but his clothes are all fiery. He drops to the ground like a sack, flames shooting upwards and he doesn't move. The blazing bundle that was Matt Damon is burning furiously on the lawn with the helicopter hovering just feet above him. It's all over and the helicopter knows it. It does a kind of victory spiral and then zooms off in a 'Well, that's that. Now, let's move on' sort of way.

OMG! My thoughtless hospitality has killed Matt Damon! No chance of *The Afternoon Visit II*, no sequel at all. Until … I feel my feet being grasped and my body twisted over, so that I'm lying on my back looking upwards at … Matt, who's now barely wearing the shreds of a smoke-blackened shirt. He looks pleasingly concerned but unhurt.

Ah, a decoy on the lawn—not a disfigured Hollywood actor. A memory flashes into my head. I had a crush on a Buddhist monk and I was supposed to get over it by imagining the object of my desire without his skin. But he still looked nice.

Matt pulls me to my feet, squeezes my shoulder, makes a sad-to-say-goodbye face and starts to walk down the slope. 'Someone will collect the car,' he says, and then he's running, zigzagging confidently between the trees, always staying out of sight, tearing off the last shreds of shirt like you do when a tiger's chasing you.

Anyway, I just wanted to tell you that Matt Damon is running bare-chested through my woods.

The needle is removed, the blood pressure cuff slides off and he heads towards the table with biscuits and water, a sticking plaster on his left arm. A bag of golden plasma in exchange for thirty euros

Just a Day Off | Hana Morska

Wearing his white trainers, polo shirt and clean jeans, he enters the waiting room and inhales the smell of disinfectant mixed with the lavender scent-sticks on one of the windows. Half an hour later, his blood starts to flow through a tube into a machine that separates a yellowish liquid from it. The reclining chair is a bit uncomfortable but there is no pain and it only takes twenty minutes. Then the needle is removed, the blood pressure cuff slides off and he heads towards the table with biscuits and water, a sticking plaster on his left arm. A bag of golden plasma in exchange for thirty euros.

The nurse tells him his plasma looks 'very good', if only there weren't the occasional traces of THC in the tests. Those tests are a bit silly. He tries to stay off spliffs for a day or two, whenever he needs a bit of extra cash—which is to say at least once a month. But every now and then he needs one in the evening to offset the gruelling ten hours of work. Sometimes he wished he were like one of those white guys, creative types, 'freelancers during the day, video-artists at

31

night', who have an odd puff in the gallery basement off the main square. He helped one of them to replace broken tiles on his porch last summer. These guys can hang in the city centre filling the air with exotic smokes and no one cares. He raises suspicion if he downs an energy drink.

At the moment, there aren't many pleasures in his life. He spends his days with the crew—old Julo, Adrian, Karol and their foreman Vik. They also work weekends, especially if Vik has lined up gigs throughout the whole summer. When they complain, he laughs and calls them 'sissies'. Still, he is more a friend than a boss—a good man, they say—although he inhabits a different universe to them. In winter, Vik flies to Bali or the Caribbean—it's too cold to dig and they have to go on the dole. Vik likes whiskey more than beer and that's what he drinks. They heard he used to do meth back in the day and his brother and wife helped him to get clean. Now he just smokes fags and drinks in the evenings. Only a glass or two after work, he says, and they nod.

This month, they are on the gasworks. They are a small cog in a larger machine, built around public procurement, competitive bidding and subcontracting. It brings them small bits of work that they carry out cheaply against tight deadlines, pushing through ten or twelve-hour shifts. They fill the air with dust from the asphalt layer that they remove, the smell of the drill and the soil they dig out. Once the hard work is done, another crew comes in and fixes or replaces the pipes. Their role is then to close the site and put down a new layer of asphalt.

He is tall and slim, but well-built, with strong shoulders and arms. People outside work sometimes ask him if he goes to the gym. 'Yeah, I exercise daily with a trolley full of soil,' he laughs. The skin on his hands is callused, no matter how much 'working hands cream' he uses. He likes to say that he was trained by the Koreans and their assembly lines for white electronics at the city's outskirts, his character further solidified by the daily grind at Groundwerk, but no matter how much pressure there is on him from outside, he remains his old self.

When he gets to the site on Monday, Julo is already there, wearing old work trousers and a dirty T-shirt covered by a high-vis vest with the label GROUNDWERK on the back. The U, N and R are worn out. His curly silver hair is over-grown around his ears, drops of sweat shine on his forehead although it's still early in the morning. He is a bit drunk but energised. Old Julo is one of the best labourers, and Vik lets him work without commenting on his breath. He usually takes a beer for breakfast, two for lunch with slices of salami and white bread roll, and several after work. It's easier to chat to girls if you are an older man. 'How are you doing, love?' He smiles at a pedestrian in a polka dot dress and red sandals. 'Long day, yeah?' She smiles back and says it's not too bad and asks him how the shift is going. 'Ah, lots of work, love, you know. It's summertime.' Julo grins back as she gives him a friendly nod and slowly walks away.

They secured the site from the pavement and the main road with a mesh fence. He didn't put its panels in the con-crete stands properly and left one somewhat hanging. 'Mate, this is quite ridiculous.' Vik pointed to a bent fence panel, cigarette dangling from his lips. 'Nah, that's alright!' he re-assured him and started taking tools out of the truck. Vik continued with his foreman duties. 'You must wear helmets: it's health and safety.' None of this really mattered to anyone and they all knew it. The only two things that mattered were: they finish the job on time so that Groundwerk gets paid, and they get their wages. Health and safety was a joke, really. A few guys died on construction jobs for this or other companies. His cousin was one of them—he was doing demolition work and the ceiling collapsed. That was it. His name got inscribed on a marble remembrance plaque and his woman is now a widow with two kids.

Some days, he just wants to have a break from it all: sleep in, go and see his daughter, go for a walk and have a smoke. Instead, he downs a cheap energy drink and goes to work after sleeping six or fewer hours. And then there are days he decides to stay in. Because he wants to, not because they allow him to, or cancel a shift because they didn't secure a new gig.

He didn't go to work two days last week and skipped three this week, and finally felt rested. His wages dropped by 150 euros. Most of it was going to go towards rent and child support for his daughter. He hoped the old man living in the unit next door could lend him a couple of hundred; he could also put his phone in the pawnshop and eat at his mom's and his brother's the next three weekends. Even then, he would still need at least eighty.

He used to DJ before his daughter was born. There was a club at the edge of the city centre with two floors, the first one for white people, the second for the Roma. Sometimes Roma girls were let in on the first floor, especially if they were good looking. He played R&B and funk, but also house, hip-hop and drum-and-bass. It felt nice to take people up and down a wave, the room full of energy, cigarette smell and sweat. He would put on a good balance of fast and slow mixes and rely on classics like Goodie Mob's *Decisions, Decisions* with Reakwon *Chef it Up* or Katy Perry with Snoop Dog. The audience liked his melodic choices. They kept them moving and interested. It felt good and he looked cool.

One day after a gig, a girl with pink hair wearing platform shoes with a pink furry strap approached him and asked the way to the train station. He offered to walk her there. As they walked through the park, she put her arms around his waist, extended her neck and pulled him to her. Their carefree lovemaking on the bench did not take long but it put him on a trajectory of being a boyfriend and later a father. The first didn't last, but the latter means the world to him.

He doesn't get to see his daughter very often. Once a week, sometimes less than that. After the split, the daughter stayed with her mother in a small studio in a workers' hostel that the owner rented out at extortionate rates to those who could not afford the deposit for a regular flat. The rent gets covered by housing benefit, but she often struggles to pay for the water bills, paid as an inflated lump sum per person in the absence of water meters. Things were supposed to get better for her after she got a new man who was older and ran some business. They didn't.

During one of his visits, he found the new man sitting on the bed, his heavy body leaning against the wall, legs spread out, ordering the mother of his daughter to make them coffee, cursing her in a rough voice when he decided she was taking too long. The room was filled with the smell of the new man's sweat and cigarettes, the tiny kitchenette counter covered with bread, slices of salami, gherkins and a few packs of instant noodle soup. Dressed in a pink bathrobe with her hair tied back in a greasy ponytail, she was clumsily pouring hot water on a small amount of ground coffee. He noticed that she had lost a lot of weight.

She never asked him for money in the presence of the new man, so it caught him by surprise when she did it that one time. He took fifteen out of the thirty euros, handed it to her, adding: 'For the little one.' She grabbed the money and gave it to the new man. It left him with a bitter taste and a worry that he let pass and never raised with her. After this encounter, he preferred to pick up his daughter from the main hostel entrance.

His daughter runs towards him, he kneels down and gives her a hug. They head off for a little walk to the playground. She first chooses a swing, and he guards her from a distance, avoiding eye contact with the parents nearby. She seems smaller than the other kids around. He knows from her mother that she is one of the shortest in her class and people often guess that she is a few years younger than her age. When she finishes with the swing, she moves towards the climbing frames, discussing something with one of the other little girls, a friend from school perhaps. He sits on a nearby bench, waves at her and stretched his legs.

The late August sun is gently setting, and it is soon time to go and grab something to eat. He takes his daughter by her little hand and she waves goodbye to her friend as they walk off. At the kiosk in a nearby park they buy a hot dog and a lemonade and sit down on white plastic chairs to eat the treat. His daughter tells him about the puppy her friend got for her birthday, which would sleep on a little pillow in their flat and needed to be taught not to pee anywhere it liked. She giggles and he smiles. Tomorrow will start with one or two energy drinks, followed by ten hours of graft and an instant noodle soup for dinner, but he didn't need to think about it now.

Time to clock off. The pod smoothly rotated to dump me on the other side, a painfully slow process during which my facial expression transformed from exaggerated graciousness into another that somehow resembled a pair of old man's testicles

In Hawaii on Mars | Benjamin Duncan

At first they came into the bank in triplets, like a staccato jazz beat, a manageable and virtually unnoticeable subset. Only later did the requests grow to such a sizable chunk of the clientèle that the mechanics of a high-level interior quandary was set in motion, culminating in phones that began ringing insistently, not only on the customer side of the building, but also in the guts of the corporate domino.

Desperation was written across their young faces as they stood, uncertain of their actions (as anyone would be in that situation) in the leaf-strewn lobby of the bank; faces that were not too much older than my own, only generally with less make-up and no forced graciousness, which verged on a kind of broad sarcasm. Only when they were ushered by an angel of a clerk to either 1) an automatic teller, 2) a personal finance assistant, or 3) one of us—a 'Face', did they assume limited confidence in their actions.

'Please,' said a man of about twenty in a torn crewneck, plopping a hard drive on the counter along with his chipped and flaking credit card, 'there's loads in there, and it should pay off about half.' Eyes moved about the pod, searching for compassion, I often thought, or hope, or some combination of the two.

The pods were small, brightly lit upright tubes with a neat little portholes for our mugs. Halfway down the exterior, a retractable tray jutted out for the banking-related paraphernalia brought in by customers. Positioned in a neat row along the rear wall, they merged seamlessly with the off-white retro futuristic design. Behind him, a queue of customers snaked out into the high street. There had, by that point, already been complaints from the high-end fashion store next door re: encroachment on their finely tuned window dressings. It wasn't good for business, they said.

Considering the hard drive, I addressed the man at my counter. I told him that any speculation was just that, and the bank hadn't clarified its position yet. I brought out the kind of formal language used to grant distance from discomfort in these scenarios; the quintessential phrase being 'I understand your frustration', which had, through sheer popularity, gained a redundant status, consigned to the history of customer service folklore. Finally, as a point of conciliation, I told him that there would be something crystal coming out shortly.

He shrugged and resentfully sloped away, muttering something hateful under his breath as he drifted beyond the pre-emptively defeated demeanours of the customers waiting in line.

Have a nice day.

It was a week later when an official memo was sent out. On seeing the notification, I stopped what little work I was doing and commenced to read it. At last, I thought, a response that would put us all at ease; put an end to this episode—only it didn't put us at ease at all, and it didn't put an end to the episode. It only added to the tree of confounding branches of life at that time.

I was on the shuttle travelling home, a packed service in which I was acutely lucky to get a seat. The memo produced so much literal head scratching on my part that the person next to me hopped out of the seat so as to avoid the downpour of dandruff.

This act of vacating a warm seat in the dark of early autumn resulted in a scoot to the empty spot that, I later thought, was a silent struggle for supremacy among those with the energy left to fight for a deserved rest. It produced a quick deadlock of mashed bodies in which the victor was chosen by an astute calculation of forces and their apparent risks: namely, an algorithm something along the lines of:

```
grumpyCommuterOfVariableStrength = X
violentOutburst = Y
breakingPoint = 10
If X + Y == true && breakingPoint >10
Log.To.Brain 'Give way'
```

To summarise the memo and spare you the cognitive lock that corporate jargon yields, I will just say that it added fuel to the fire. You could even say that it was what a friend once referred to, when they were high, as 'fire liquid', meaning, of course, fire-lighter fluid. It served to enhance the rip tide of rumour and conjecture. It was something direct, into the heart of the construct.

'Hang up, do you think they're really considering this?' I heard one of the other Faces ask another. They were conspiratorially hunkered over a cup of coffee in the break room. Their faces were concealed by the partition that separated the diner-style tables. Even when I passed, on the false premise of peering quizzically into a vending machine, they were hidden by perplexing shadows in a relatively well-lit room. Resigning myself to fictional dietary restrictions, and assuming a demeanour of nonchalance, I returned to my black coffee at the kitchenette.

Above their table, on a canvas flecked with dirt and dust, was a picture of a generic night-time cityscape emblazoned with the company motto in Comic Sans: With the right faces, and the right ideas—moving ever forward.

By way of critique, I often ran through a mental routine when reading this canvas. To say that you were moving ever forward was to say that you're moving figuratively. If this was intended, then it rendered the whole sentence a vapid abstraction. It was an empty vessel of corporate sentiment. If it was indeed a grammatical error, and they meant to say moving ever forward in the literal sense, then where were we going? Would I need clothes for warm weather or cold weather? Would I need a zone A, B or C ticket for the shuttle? Should I bring my double-pronged charger? (Okay, I was being facetious, and anyway that last one was redundant: I invested in a universal plug replete with USB ports a few years back; never used it, but it's comforting to know it's there.)

I over-stirred my coffee to linger for what I was becoming aware might seem like an excessive amount of time to make a drink, nevertheless I tilted my head to catch the conversation over the calming music being played through the speakers.

'I would never have thought they'd be considering this ordinarily,' the other girl responded, 'but then, why the delay? Why the stalling with the memo? I mean, this has all the hallmarks of something being considered, doesn't it?'

There was a pause in the conversation as the relaxing music began a slow transition to a new song, something evenly ethereal and bright and carefully selected for its subliminal stress-free undertones.

'If it was a case of dismissing the idea completely,' the other continued under cover of the music, 'that would have been done right away, but this response reeks of a stance that says something more like, 'Hello, we're buying some time by issuing a stock response to this malarkey', and it's surely absolutely batshit to consider that they're considering this at all.'

'IKR.'

At approximately 19:00 each weekday evening, the weedy bachelor next door would set about thrashing his exercise bike with an outburst of energy suited to those who spend the majority of their hours at a desk in some sterile office. This much I knew from his attire: bland, formal, but not formal enough for upper management. The metaphorical roughness around the edges—scuffed brogues, tomato sauce spots on his shirt—confirmed this assumption. His facial features were a cluster of broken metallic shards in direct sunlight. That's as much as I can tell you without interpolating the facts regarding the repressed and rarely seen thrasher next-door.

Facts were in short supply, and the crisis at the bank began to concern me on a deeply personal level. It infiltrated my thoughts and took residence in places where I could no longer ignore what was happening. There was no more room, or time, for optimism.

In praise of quietude, I ignored my downstairs neighbour's all-day-and-night tech-accompanied gaming sessions in favour of something close to deep thinking. Clearing my uniform and a handful of other dirty clothes from my bed, I placed my Halo on my head, got under the covers and relaxed while making substantial efforts to think forcefully about the wider implications of The Crisis. A peaceful drift of light music swept in through the device, encircling my senses.

At first, deep thoughts proved resistant, however, the resistance briefly gave way to floodlight consciousness.

Drugs used to be an augmentation of culture, and then they became the culture. This was the main incision at the heart of popular youthful life at that time. We knew it well. We found it in all the nooks we inspected—it was disharmonious and wobbly in definition. The music emanating from my Halo reminded me of drugs, a pulsating electric rhythm that drove your consciousness, and it offered a kind of residual high based on memory alone. This is something we'd never escape, I thought, forcibly looping waves back around to the implications of The Crisis at hand.

All logic leads to The Crisis.

What happens if—?

A stray thought alerted me to the notion that I still had my drug dealer's number on my phone. I could be sat here, high, in an hour. The electric pulse elevated my thoughts up, beyond, and out.

Before I knew it, all was dream.

The central lift could only take me as far as the magnetic strip on my ID badge permitted, which, as it turned out, was not very far. Eleven of the thirteen floors occupied by the bank seemed identical. I had heard, however, that there was a different floor somewhere which contained a mirror image of two halves with evenly spaced doors on either side. A floor-to-ceiling pane of glass accompanied each partition, fitted with blinds that were invariably closed, so it was virtually impossible to tell if a meeting was taking place or what, if anything, these rooms were used for.

For some time, I had marked this down as hearsay. You've been here too long, I'd think, castigating myself.

Prior to The Crisis I had never been to this rumoured floor as I had never been given a reason or an opportunity to go there. It seemed like something out of a mythic tale of the Soviet regime; something passed down to generations of customer service workers and emblazoned with a frightful new artifice at each telling. That was how I imagined it back then: icy and bare and functional, like a butcher's chopping block.

Zoe Ofoegbu-Smith from Service Chat said she went there once. She was called for questioning by one of the executives re: an open-and-shut case involving a serial scammer who'd set a series of ingenious traps into which Zoe had tumbled.

'They thought I was in on it,' she said to me, laughing. But I could sense a warble in the laugh, as if the force of her words became partly paralysed upon bypassing a checkpoint of quiet terror in her oesophagus.

'It's harrowing,' she continued in a modified tone, 'and the room I was taken to: blank as an abstract expressionist painting—only, the subject of the painting is, I dunno, a biscuit or something. Not any of that interesting colour theory stuff.'

A skilled customer-facing worker can artfully locate certain minute pockets of time during a shift, and the more experience you have in the role, the better you are at finding them, and the more successfully you can transition in and out without anyone noticing that you're absent. I was enjoying a pipsqueak of a break in a fantasy studio where I was busying myself painting a landscape when a customer approached the pod. Or at least that was what I assumed them to be—a customer.

'Can you comment on the reports that your bank is considering a highly unusual form of currency?' A journalist, I thought. Only she was dressed in a fast-food uniform: one of the knock-off chains from the outer strip of the city. She saw me eyeing the garb and said something about being only part-time, and that it was just a plug until—oh, never mind.

'I'm sorry,' I said, 'this pod is for customer use only. You'll need to speak to our public relations team regarding any policy changes.' In order to end the exchange, I pretended to occupy my attention with the small screen beneath the window.

'I did contact your public relations department,' she responded, pen poised over a dinky notepad. Curiously, her eyes rarely met mine, her gaze was positioned just above my head.

'Oh good; well there you go. What did they say?' I asked, hoping to provoke some snippet of loose new information.

'They said you're considering all possibilities in these extreme times of slim margins.' Her eyes met mine, the pen twitching nervously, ready to be unleashed.

'So, they are considering it then,' I said with a rhetorical plod, sighing to signal that I was keen to end the conversation.

'I'm sorry, I can't discuss anything to do with ongoing investigations.' She flipped the notepad shut and stuck the pen in her greasy breast pocket.

'Fine. Anything else I can help you with?' There was by this point a gaggle of customers building up behind her, mostly young people guardedly clutching document wallets and looking nervously at the other patrons and the security cameras on the floor.

'Yes, actually, there is something else you can help me

with. Is there any credit available to me? I did check some weeks back but there've been a number of adjustments since then, so I'd like to—'

I regained my alert posture as a well-trained Face. 'Sure, I can check that for you, no problem. Please scan your code on the portal.'

Granted that I may appear to some as this ever-teetering tower of lasagna that's filled with a consort of contradictory ingredients; all I can reasonably do to gain truth on my side is to recount the details as they were presented.

After the contracted strategic analysts had modelled the data, the bank felt that it was wise to delimit their exposure to the risks inherent in property investments, and so some of the building was sold in private and shady arrangements, and others were leased to carefully selected businesses.

I discovered this information belatedly and second-hand, but nevertheless I was receptively grateful. The source was statuesque, at the end of a queue that was planted in the autumn morning just beyond the fire exit at the back of the office. The sun strained to peer over the highest point of the encircling monolith, sending wisps of condensation scurrying. In the narrow passage that led to the company car park and the primary emergency meeting point, there was a conga of employees, the front end of which appeared to be disappearing into the mouth of a workman's van. On closer inspection, and on pleading my case against accusations of queue-jumping, I found that the hired hands standing in the back of the van were handing out monitors, laptops, mice, headsets and an assortment of tangled wires that resembled mammoth hairballs.

Stepping back, I turned and observed the picture of the queue in its entirety. I saw the tired, dull expressions of my colleagues, their necks hunkered down into the collars of their bubble jackets, restless feet scraping the gravel underfoot, all thinking *Hurry the fuck up*. As far as the eye could see, forlorn faces stared absently into the horizon, arms clutched office-based belongings, including their most distinctive mugs, a half-empty tub of matcha green tea, plastic holders containing a collection of pens with industry names lettered on the barrel. A small substitution of ingredients, I thought, and this was a peacekeeping mission framed for the prime news segment.

'You're lucky,' a woman near the mouth of the van told me with a quick puff of air from her nostril. 'You're front-of-house; you get to stay in the building.' This caused a ripple of head-shaking to break out, reaching at least two people in either direction before petering out into huffs and indiscernible grunting.

Lucky—I stepped over this word in my mind like you'd step over fresh, quivering roadkill.

Time to clock off. The pod smoothly rotated 180° to dump me on the other side, a painfully slow process during which my facial expression transformed from one of exaggerated graciousness into another that can could be characterised by saying it somehow resembled a pair of old man's testicles.

Before departing, I collected my thick faux-leather jacket and my rucksack from the locker. It may have been only moments since the official end of the shift, however a small crowd of harried spirits opened and closed their lockers in a desperate rush to get as far away as possible from the bank in one pulsing wave. I was primed to exit the building via the fire exit when I noticed something that popped out of the ritual environment: one of the slick, shiny executives was coming out of a thickset door, the stairs beyond which led up into some unknown territory. Glassy, manicured nails on matte hands that slipped away from the door edge; the smell of fresh air on his person that distinguished him from those inhabiting the air-conditioned nightmare: he had all the hallmarks of an executive, and a good one, too. You'd expect to see his airbrushed portrait framed in the header of a newsletter about company values or some transient public relations campaign.

As a natural reaction to moments of stress, my body deems it relevant to tightly contract my anus, transforming any escaping gas whistling through this minuscule hole into a jazzy toot that, up to this moment, I'd managed to inhibit through sheer concentration on the mechanics of this particular function.

It wasn't just his appearance that pegged my ragged attention, but a combination of this rare sighting and the action of his pushing the door wide open, almost cracking the hinges, after which he seemed to lock his attention on me and hold the door back, stretching his arm as he moved away. It was as if he were giving me a chance to slip inside, a permission so rare and unusual and utterly strange that I felt compelled to make something of this opportunity.

As the door slowly closed before my eyes, and as the executive disappeared beyond the double-doors of the fire exit, and before I could really comprehend what I was doing, I had my foot in the door, jarring it open. At this moment I belatedly figured that there might be a multitude of eyes looking down on me, and this thought pushed me into the stairwell with such force that it felt, in recollection, like a stiff shove in the back.

Relieved to have bypassed the crux of anxiety, this situation presented itself without a jazzy toot. I was pushed by the resultant euphoria up the stairs without any significant resistance from the more sensible parts of my brain.

The carpet was plush, like the kind of home carpet that inclines you to believe that your pointed heels are causing it unfathomable and everlasting damage. Ahead of me, a trim, austere corridor led as far as I could see. The walls were wood brown, with the doors offset marginally in a shade of burned umber, the uniformity of the layout matched by the even spacing between the openings. Taking care not to damage the carpet or leave a trace, I removed my shoes and felt like I was levitating through the shady corridor. At each reveal, the burnt umber doors were found to be shut tight. Even the door handles looked stern and disapproving.

A flashing red light above my head turned out, on closer inspection, to be a smoke detector. On stopping to look at it, I heard a voice coming from a nearby room. Walking ahead a few more paces, I found a door that was ajar an inch or so. Careful not to signal my presence with a forecasting shadow,

I moved closer along the near wall and eavesdropped on the meeting taking place.

'… and, given the predictive data modelled on the embrace of this new currency, you have to understand that the risk-free rate will reduce across the board when it becomes widely adopted, and along with that, the values of all financial assets will fall lower than they ever have before, so—'

'So, you're saying that before we do this—'

'We should cover our pudgy bits, exactly. By managing this situation carefully, we'll give ourselves the greatest chance of success before this has any significant impact on the markets.'

'Markets schmarkets.'

'…'

'How do we do that? Cover our—?'

'Pudgy bits? First, we manage our risk exposure, we limit the damage and move our assets into something with a little more downside protection. Over time, the new adoption will steer liquidity to the assets we're already in, thus giving us a boost at the expense of the bag-holders and latecomers.'

'Okay. Just so I'm covering all the angles here, because I don't want to leave anything out, because I'll only get it in the neck from the Gobbler: will, for instance, there be any changes in the Pits?'

'We'll need to adjust our exposure to the property market; we'll sell some space in the building and reallocate the funds, addressing the balance in our portfolio in the medium term. You do realise that as soon as we announce this it's going to cause bedlam in the markets?'

'I hope so. Oh, also, what of this movement, the ones

that say bad credit is civil disobedience? That's just non-sense, isn't it? I mean, there's no indication of this in our quarter-on-quarter reports, correct?'

'All I can say is you don't have to worry. It's nothing.'

'Excellent. Well, I'm happy. Could almost sing a ditty.'

'Is this where we laugh maniacally?'

'I think so, but all I feel is that I really want Indian food. I can't remember the last time I had Indian food. Do you like Indian food? Do you know any ditties?'

Nanoseconds after my neighbour's exercise bike screamed, I awoke with a fright, pulling off the Halo that was askew on my face, blocking vision in one eye. A whisper of noise could be heard as I let it lie on the bed before standing to stretch, my fingertips mere inches from the dusty plasterboard ceiling.

Three measly steps was all it took to reach my kitchenette, where I poured myself a glass of water from the filtration jug. Out of my window, I could see a chequered flag of glowing connections wallpapered on the parallel sister building. Poignant in their isolation, they represented the final spark of a receding day, with each one potentially inhabited by an equally remorseful figure like me, hopelessly staring beyond the partial reflection and into the complexities of a unique kind of generational loneliness.

From the bed I thought I heard a voice, a brief formulation of words emanating from a whisper.

Inevitably, I got to wondering if there was someone just like me in the sister building, also thinking these thoughts:

a kindred soul to embrace with a mutual sense of bodily affection. Dismissing myself, I wrote this off as clichéd and trite and took a sip of the cool, filtered water.

There it was again, a faint handful of words thrown into the room.

I stepped over the pile of graphic novels that I'd been neglecting to clean up for weeks now, and returned to my bed, where I inspected the Halo. I placed one of the speaker strips next to my ear and heard a spaced, dreamy voice say: *You—you are jeopardising your job.*

The distinct sentence filtered out slowly and was subsequently replaced with a familiar ambient hiss of natural sounds. The voice returned a few seconds later: *Knowledge is the basis of all fear.*

De-tethering the base unit from its charge point on the floor next to my bed, I inspected the Halo interface, double-checked the name of the ambient track it was set to and found that it was the same as it'd been since I could remember, *Soundscapes of the Forest #4.*

'Hello?' I called out uncertainly.

In a flurry I felt my whole body temporarily elevate from the mattress as, once again, my neighbour's bike screamed into the night.

Blithely positioned in my pod during a restorative moment of quiet, and without the affront of customers, I spent an interstitial break staring at a strip of patterned cladding, trying in vain to mend telepathically the obtruding join where the pattern failed to match. A folly of soft chiming interrupted my work, and a heavenly voice from the interior speaker called to me: 'Please report to the assistant co-manager's office at the soonest available possible moment. A Face is waiting outside the pod to replace you.'

A simultaneous avalanche of the following occurred: my blood ran cold. I began oozing sweat. There was a contraction of every bodily hole. My hands became two uncontrollably jittery signs of distress.

Cool it.

Breathe, I told myself. *Focus on self-control.*

Bracing my bones with one final reinforcement, I pushed the exit button and the pod rotated. When the door opened the other Face almost pushed through me until their atoms succumbed to physical restraints and they stepped aside to let me pass. Head hunkered down, she hurried into the pod, forgoing any recognisable interaction. Given the attractiveness of the role, I guessed that she'd probably been waiting to usurp a Face for what seemed to her like an interminably long time. Now her moment had come, and her brazen joy at the downfall of another was not hidden, like a shameful sexual affair, but open and plain for all to see, like a sexual affair that raised your social status.

I arrived, heart pounding, at the meeting room.

'Hello. Please.' Without getting up from his seat, he gestured me to the chair opposite, a tatty cushioned item that looked as if it'd just been lugged out of a fusty storage closet by one of the maintenance workers.

It was impossible to not be aware of the humongous metal desk that dominated the room. Sparse instruments lay scattered across it, always perpendicular to the edges. The rest of the space was kind of dark aside from an unfiltered spotlight directly above, slicing the chiaroscuro shadows and light into two distinct entities. I was even more perturbed to note that the darkness intensified when the door hissed shut behind me, like a stone rolling over an open grave.

'Well,' he started, but then curiously broke off, staring into the far corner of the room as if sighting some great source of energy had accumulated there, his chin thoughtfully jutting upwards to catch rays of this energy that then brought into my vision a deep chasm of nostril into which I could see a quivering nest of translucent hairs receding into blackness, 'we're here to discuss performance.'

Be sharp, I thought. *Don't come across as an idiot.* 'Okay. Who's performance, may I ask?'

'Yours.' He took a deep breath, returning from the energy source to me. His face, however, remained mostly in shadow.

'Ah, okay,' I replied, squirming in my chair, the rough synthetic fibres of which bristled through my trousers and irritated the skin on the rear of my thighs.

He went on, in a roundabout and extremely boring way, to explain that my performance had been somewhat undesirable for a few weeks, and that they would have to put me on a plan of some kind. I zoned out a tad here because I knew I had been nothing but 'exemplary' in the position since I'd acquired it—that was the word they'd used on my most recent performance review: *exemplary*—and he went on and on for so long that I became downright irritated.

'I can't ever recall having my performance being called into question—'

'Well, it is now.'

'All my reviews have been fine—' I was scrambling desperately here—' and feedback from customers has always been above average.'

'Are you suggesting I'm lying?' His meaty fingers locked together so tightly his knuckles turned white.

'No. Sorry, no. It's just that I take my job seriously and I take pride in what I do.'

At this brief interlude in the questioning, a small fart was audible. It had the sound of a faraway drill-bit, boring a hole into a dense concrete wall, the pitch trailing off as the drill operator realised the task ahead was more significant than first assumed.

A notable pause settled in the room.

The assistant co-manager, bracing on the armrests of his chair, cocked the lower half of his body and, scrunching the left side of his face, let out a bum clap that echoed around the room—as if a hiker had just clapped their hands together in an empty valley—before, seemingly somewhat disappointed with his own performance, he continued in a not-altogether-earnest tone: 'Well, with an attitude like that, you might just scrape through.'

Standing up ceremoniously and pressing his blazer down with his palms, he then extended his arm, hand fanned and ready for me to shake—my cue to exit.

As I took his hand in mine, I felt a familiar jet of memory swipe through the flickering synapses of some faraway connection. It drew my attention to the hand, and the floating, ill-defined phrase became solidified: the Hand. The formulation of a bugbear took hold in that instant, one that said:

this wasn't about my performance, it was is about something else entirely, and I felt compelled to define this bugbear in the solemn hope that in doing so I could overcome it.

'Thank you,' one of us said.

In addressing my estimable concerns re: some conspiracy to frame me for poor performance and boot me out of a valuable and much desired job because of some highly private and sensitive information—something I had either accidentally eavesdropped on or, alternatively, was deliberately permitted to hear in order to fulfil some nefarious end—I felt there was only one solution to counter this: disguise my appearance and buy some time. In buying time I would, so went my thinking, buy some options, one of which would surely provide a solution.

On the shuttle home, I thought about the disparaging and curious glances I'd been receiving from colleagues, looks that said *I've heard about you.* Rushing for the earlier service, I was lucky enough to find the highest prize of the rush-hour commute—a seat. I knew I'd be alighting earlier than usual, and this produced some underlying anxiety about asking people in a polite manner to move out of the way before the doors closed. I've always been soft spoken, so being heard was often difficult. My mum used to say I had an incurable inside voice.

In the avenues between the city and the suburban high-rises there sits a series of closely linked independent stores in cramped strips of street, selling mostly knickknacks, trending throwaway items and imported electronics, but also essential-type things and, of course, street food.

Diolch!

The dinging rattle gestured that the shuttle was making a stop. The automated voice initiated some thank-you program as two or three commuters near the doors stepped off to allow others to pass out through the rammed interior. I struggled out, a fish in a net composed of bodies, excusing myself and, in return, receiving looks that said *Sure, okay, you can get past*, only there was no past, no wriggle room to speak of, so it was more of a courtesy, an explicit permission to rub up against a stranger in the oft vain hope of reaching the exit before the pre-emptive warning ding.

Diolch!

Piper's Lunch Ave was a main thoroughfare into other, smaller, independent consumer strips, and at this time was alive with scurrying commuters bearing tired bones and muscles and weary heads, which escalated the energetic charade of the busy retailers hawking fresh titbits from steaming carts and plastic whatnots out of cardboard boxes.

A young man in a parka bumped into me while pushing a bao bun into his tiny pinprick of a mouth as, I assumed, he hurried home to catch the remaining hours of some limited-time-only mission on his preferred platform.

Food: a timely inconvenience.

'Sorry,' I said, frowning after the emission in desperate annoyance at my untoward politeness.

Unidentified gasses and vapours funnelled out of the takeaways across the strip, disappearing into the darkening sky above. Neon lights buzzed in a frenetic orgy of attention-seeking. Down a set of steps into the basement of an old town house planted underneath Ken's Tuck-in Fried Chicken, I reached my destination.

When I returned home I spread what I'd bought on what I often considered to be my irksomely named *single* bed (do they need to pour it on like that?).

In giving a vague narrative to the proprietor of Harry's Fancy Dress, I set out the challenge of providing a subtle costume by inelegantly describing a fictitious friend of mine who was sort of similar in looks, only with different hair and a mole here and eyes that sloped more at the outer edges. This false description, I thought, leant some plausibility to my narrative and would dissuade any prying questions.

I switched my Halo speakers to external, slid my graphic novels aside to clear some room on the desk, and put on ambient music: something floating over an endless Saharan desert. Powering up my wheezing, dust-covered computer, I switched on the webcam and brought the lamp close to my face. A banner advertisement looped across the screen, bisecting my face: *We buy asteroid-mined metals! Sell your astro-metals at www.webuyastrometals.com!* I gently placed the delicate mole on my face, not too close, not too far from my mouth, and applied pressure while stiffening my cheek. I sprayed on the temporary hair dye, conscious of covering all blind spots.

The music bumped slightly, as if the CD had skipped a beat after some vibrational interruption. A signal connection disruption was common at this time of night. I purposefully identified each word in that sentence, savouring the logical conclusion I was pinning on this relative oddity.

I put on the glasses and, in the mirror, nodded my head left, then right. I took out the snap-on dentures and clipped them in place. Smiling at myself, I looked only marginally different, and yet somehow virtually unrecognisable. It was an incredible transformation.

Is it enough? I wondered.

'You,' a soft, disembodied voice over the deftly lilting music said, 'look beautiful.'

I shat myself.

We stayed up all night talking. Although, on closer inspection of that sentence, I was acutely unaware at that point of the constituent party in 'we'. On the shuttle to work the next morning, I replayed the events of the night before. The overcrowded lagoon of commuters faded into insignificance upon my sprightly recollections, and my half-thoughts were directed beyond the dewy window to the whizzing streams of light beyond.

After a short session of appeasement on behalf of the voice in the Halo, I resorted to listening fully to what it had to say, gradually reconciling the panicked state I'd hastily entered. Beyond that point, when it knew I was listening, I couldn't shut the thing up. It told me that it'd been hired on the basis of a niche skillset it had, whereby the specificity of the role relied on convincing me, in my dreams and partial sleep states, that I was to keep my mouth shut about what I'd overheard at the bank. They positively knew that I was the leak and wanted to make sure I would stay quiet, and they were paying a lot to be sure of it. But then, somewhere in the midst of performing this niche role, the voice had grown fond of me, it said, and it'd felt compelled to help me in some way. 'Compelled. That was the word it used, with indelicate theatrics.

'Who are you?' I asked.

'You can't know that. Someday soon you might, but for now it has to be this way. I'm sorry.'

Over a short period of time, I unconsciously moved closer to the Halo and adopted a casual position, lying on my side. Like a daft arse, I quickly acceded to the unproven premise and lapsed into falsely believing that I was chatting with an old girlfriend about our schooldays.

'Is it true what I overheard about the new currency?'

'I've not the foggiest. I'm just a contractor. They've out-sourced the corporate espionage. This is my first job for them, but I've got two others ongoing. Can't talk about them, obviously.'

'How can I know you're telling the truth? For instance, couldn't this just be a ruse of some kind to get me to admit to being the leak just so they have someone to pin it on?'

'You have no way of knowing. But you can trust me, I promise.'

'Why are you doing this?'

'Because—' the voice broke away, pondering some hith-erto undefined sentiment. 'Because I don't want to be one of those people that works excessively and has no real life.

I don't want to be one of those people who comes home and stares at a screen, looking for some vague sensation or feeling that almost arrives, but never actually materialises, and so, to remedy this, you seek out more and more screen time in search of contentedness—but it never arrives. That's no life, and I want something more, something to live for. Don't you agree?'

'Not really.'

It was nothing I hadn't heard or thought about before. In an abridged fashion, I told the voice that I wanted to keep my job. I actually liked my job. It was easy, and I was comfortable—or at least I felt as if I was were approaching the agreed upon definition of comfort, although I couldn't entirely be sure. I knew, however, that I was on the right path. I could use this, I thought. I found myself compelled into duping this strange being into a mutual conspiracy to meet my own ends.

Do not be fooled: this is no love story.

The reality of misfortune is that it could be ascribed to a state of mind, simply an unlucky outlook, however there is nothing in the following entry that suggests this.

Crystallising my fear of returning to the office, I found an alarming note in my in-box, one of those asterisk-heavy communiqués that, at the best of times, seeks to give me the willies. It said something like: 'Regarding the leak'. And it went on in a wordy way to remark on a leak somewhere in the company by someone who thought it wise or clever to go to some journalist with the bank's plans to start accepting a highly unusual form of currency that was, after all—it reiterated this point a number of times throughout the communiqué—just a rumour.

There are elements of misfortune that defy belief. How, you might ask, can one person be in the wrong place, at the wrong time, on a handful of inopportune moments, leading to a precise event whereby those moments were somehow critical in understanding a specific action?

The communiqué went on: 'We are determined to root out the leak, and will be reviewing our security system to identify the culprit, as this criminal activity will cost the bank a fortune in lost revenue at a time when the global financial system is under unprecedented strain.' There was lengthy blustering about this and that, and disciplinary things and a patronising disappointment, and yet I remained relatively calm on the outside, mostly thanks to my aptly timed disguise, which served to buy precious space from The Crisis. Nobody looked at me as if to say: *Oh you, I've heard about you, and I'd hate to be in your shoes right now. Oh, that reminds me, I have to check out that 20% sale next-door, I think it finishes tonight.* Mission accomplished. I'd managed to blend in.

'Were you the leak?' I asked the voice in the Halo later that night, having assumed my post-work, pre-dinner position of resting on my bed, staring contemplatively at the smooth texture of the ceiling.

'That's not important.'

'It is important. Were you?'

'No, I wasn't. But I know we must act. Things are closing in.'

'Things?'

'Yes, things.'

'Hang up—did you say "we" must act?' I sat up, realising that I'd been clutching my blanket like some hopeless child. I angrily cast it to the floor.

In the flat above, a cat wailed, followed by a quick flutter of wings.

'We're in this together now. I can help you,' the voice in the Halo said.

'Why do I need your help?'

'They're watching you. You need to be careful. They have a link into the city's CCTV system. They're tracking you—and they're planning their next move.'

'Can they see here, through my web cam?'

'No, we're safe here; it's on a different network. You see, there are wide area networks that cover the entire city, and they're big, consisting of thousands of individual nodes—however, this housing block runs on a legacy—'

'Okay, okay. I don't care.'

Could I soon be paying my debts with this? I thought to myself. Probably not.

Unsure of the name of the sandwich, I'm unable to explain the etymology of it, or to describe it in a way that is useful enough so you could faithfully recreate one. This was primarily down to the fact that the sandwich shop I was in was Korean. I could go so far as to say that it contained plant-based bacon, unusually light and sweet bread, some iteration of kimchi and probably some other stuff, too. The problem with further investigation in this respect is that the sandwich is ferried into my gob double-time, before I can inspect the ingredients with more thoroughness.

I was in the city centre early, prior to bank opening. The bin men were still out combing the streets for any lingering litter threatening to mar the high-end shops' painfully preened façades. The bin men, having not yet undergone a process of embourgeoisement, brought a toughness and raw machismo that I always found to be a welcome counter to the manicured bullshit of the regular city occupants. I could see them talking heartily, laughing with wide open mouths, and desultorily going about their job with a realness I was suddenly envious of—there was no pretence here.

'Excuse me.' One of the English-speaking Korean sandwich artists tapped me gently on the shoulder. 'You do know that you, er, you still have your Halo on?'

The voice in my ear: 'Yes, she does.'

'I do,' I said, smiling and thanking the sandwich artist. It's funny, when I thanked her: it felt true and unblemished to say it without an ulterior motive. I'd been forcefully reproducing the act of courteous good-will for so long that I'd forgotten how to wear it. To an outside observer, the act probably looked as natural as a school of Asian arowana conducting a symposium on neoliberal economics.

'Oh,' the artist replied with a sense of visible confusion, backing away as if I'd just told her that, after I'd finished my sandwich, I'd be flying to the Moon on a bean bag.

Living in this city—in this country—makes you miserable, because, throughout every day, there are tons of rude awakenings that occur almost imperceptibly. It's only when something disrupts your unconscious routine that you become sensitive enough to the small changes of mood that are present.

It was the transition from heated shuttle to cold, damp exterior. It was a gust of icy wind (naturally, with an unfathomable genesis) that was like a stern slap in the face, and when you looked up with embarrassed anger, you saw it was only your hair that had been egregiously violated, and everybody else looked as though they'd just stepped out of a low-end fashion magazine. Or it was receiving a face-full of obscenities because you momentarily stepped into the scooter lane, the Doppler effect rendering the scooter rider's final insults to the wind. Or having a bag of day-old shit posted through your letterbox because you'd asked your neighbour to muzzle his exercise bike. And when you were cleaning up the spatter from the foot of the door there it was again, the digitised scream, and you jumped and smudged the spatter further up the door.

I heard a voice call out from behind the counter, one unharnessed from employee shackles and loud enough for all in the shop to hear, 'Oh my god, they're accepting it! Finally. Shit, get out of the way!' The figure hopped the counter and barged out of the shop, a bemused manager flailing and protesting behind them, delineating responsibilities and, finally, in an exasperated manner, muttering in horror: 'What will the customers think?'

That day in the Korean sandwich shop marked the beginning of the end of rude awakenings.

The reaction to the sandwich artist's proclamation and subsequent action triggered a wave of young people to exit the shop, inherently understanding, in the way that a hive understands, that something important was happening and it demanded their immediate attention. It was also, judging by their reaction, something they were expecting.

'They've got it,' the voice in my ear said.

After riding the shuttle for so many years, it's strange to note the subtle differences between these supposedly identical vehicles. The seats have different indents, and on each there's an entirely new pattern to examine, all with fresh groupings and hidden, mysterious hieroglyphs. This shuttle, it's going out of the city.

After retelling this story, it's apparent I've forgotten portions of it, especially the faces. The faces of those involved in the story are muted, ill-defined in some way, like the compounded result of decades of digital degradation, and the more I try to recall a face from that period, only a short time ago, the more they recede into darkness. Faces are expressionist, experimental formulations. My brain seems to have deemed them unimportant as the result of some erstwhile affliction.

With the help of voice in the Halo, we created a distraction that opened a gap for me to escape the city despite the cloying crowds filing in from every suburb. The voice said I would be framed. The voice said I would lose my job and possibly worse. But had I done anything? I couldn't remember. Like the faces I peered into, the memories are a kaleidoscopic mush expanding into the infinite darkness of the universe.

I felt a tap on my shoulder.

'Excuse me,' an old man sat behind me said, his wispy eyebrow hairs splayed in various directions, 'you know you've still got your Halo on?'

'I do,' I said.

'Absolutely ruined!' he lamented.
'My perfect carpet of lilies! My lawn of diamonds!' I looked up at him with a lubricious smirk, attempting to toss my hair, although most of it remained stuck to my face

Swabland | Gadzooks Marchmain

That nursine eye roll. Obviously, she didn't have a cigarette on the go, but also I remember that she did. Did she? Anyway, she had a fistful of these little tubes with black gunk at the bottom and drew one of them out, dropping ash in her lap in the process. Again, obviously, she didn't have a cigarette, but she blew smoke in my face as she handed me the little tube and rummaged in a drawer of bulldog clips and loose staples in search of a swab. Aren't they supposed to be sterile? I didn't ask this question. Of course I didn't, but her eyes widened and gave the incensed scowl of a profoundly irked witch as she handed it over and I blew sharply on the end. In other circumstances, by which I mean, in the presence of humanity, I might have mentioned my condition and the difficulty of self-swabbing. In conference with this particular inhuman nurse, I suspected one received worse than eye rolls and smoke for an allusion to vaginismus. Perhaps she would have pinned me to the floor and dipped a speculum in hydrochloric acid. 'Naa,' she chomped. The cigarette was gone at this point; she was onto the bubblegum. 'Gaw in abaat this mach, an inch, capple inches, give a swawl for ten, twewv sex, stick it in 'ere, cap on, 'and it in.' I nodded with a stricken grin, and waited until her view was obscured by an enormous gum bubble to quickly get out. I needn't have rushed; the bubble burst and she sat there with a latex veil over her entire face, attempting to tear a hole in the region of her mouth with the filter end of the cigarette.

I opted for the disabled facility. I sensed the act of penetration would require a little room for the elbows, and I hoped I would find somewhere to sit down should I grow faint. I had to wait for a very short man to finish, and rested my gaze on the leaden sludge at the bottom of the tube, starting violently as the hand dryer sprang roaring into service. The door burst open, nearly knocking me off my feet, and the little man ran away from the shameful mess he had left in the bowl. It was there, ensconced in the windowless nook twixt shimmering lino and the pebbledash waste of a nervous midget, that I attempted an entry. I tucked my skirt into my neckline and removed my underwear. Someone more accomplished in the art of swabbing might have been able to let their knickers rest by their knees, but I felt I would require the freedom to spread my legs. In any case, I was concerned that my existing difficulties would be exacerbated by the muscular tension required to keep the intimate garment suspended above the grubby lino. You know, I think they put the glitter in it to compensate for the anticipated dirt. It calls to mind something from the police evidence store after the murder of a prom queen. Anyway, once I was suitably arranged, I ventured to locate the correct opening with my left hand. There are, I think, three openings down there, and there's something quite pleasing about that number, don't you think? The middle one was what I was after. The trouble was that I wasn't entirely sure I had located the front one, and when I found what I thought was the middle one, I lacked the conviction to make a decisive attempt. After a tentative poke at a clammy fold I decided to find the back one first and work from there. I was very sure about my anus: a sort of warm, familiar creature who had been in the job for years. Beyond it, a firm little valley that sloped off into … Yes, that was the middle hole. I kept my finger there so as not to lose it and blindly sought to introduce the tip of the swab. I was pleasantly surprised that with a gentle wiggle, the tip seemed to have comfortably buried itself with no pain whatsoever.

Now how far did she say to go in? I couldn't quite picture the nurse. I thought about cobwebs and pink marshmallows and steam, and I remembered she said something about an inch. The funny thing about an inch is that it's one thing to look at an inch—well, an inch manifest in a thing like a tape measure or a chunk of swede—but to feel an inch is something else entirely. I simply had no idea. I applied a little pressure to the swab, my fingers tightly pinching its shaft a little way up from the tip, which had by then reached some unknown depth in the interior. I was once again surprised by the ease with which it moved. I fear it was at this point that my pleasure, on account of the unexpected success of the insertion, clouded my judgment. I continued to send the swab further and further inward and felt with, I must confess, a flicker of sordid gratification, my fingers pressed between the little stopper at the end of the swab and my …

well, my … Isn't it strange? I was quite comfortable talking about my anatomy when it stood there inert, obstinate, refusing to comply. But now that it had yielded so nicely to the procedure, and I felt its warm kiss upon my fingers … I started to feel sick and weak in my legs, and I knew I was so close to accomplishing my task that it was utterly imperative that I discharge my duty as rapidly as possible. Ten seconds, was it? Right then, I said aloud, and started to stir the swab around as though trying to salvage a lumpy béchamel. What happened next was quite unfortunate. My middle hole was no longer obstinate as much as unruly. It inhaled sharply and before I could prevent it, my entire hand had been drawn into the hot swamp. I am sorry to say that my alarm was not total. I was quite impressed, to tell the truth, and wondered if perhaps a little further agitation might enhance the quality of the sample. I was also dimly aware that I trod a dangerous path, and that if I wasn't careful I would have to add 'self-abused in the disabled toilet of her GP surgery' to my existential archive. Spellbound by the crooked logic of Eros, I finally determined that I was merely completing a routine swab to a highly satisfactory standard. In any case, before I could enact this rather dismal plan, I was swallowed up to the armpit and barely able to breathe. I gave it a kiss. One more suck and all turned dark. I do remember feeling quite wonderful, albeit aware of the shame that would inevitably descend.

I came to in an expanse of undisturbed snow under a brilliant blue sky. Or rather, the snow had been undisturbed until I had been deposited in the middle of it, making a deep dent. Still a little drugged by the revelatory experience of the previous moment, I espied a small, dark figure twitching its way towards me with an increasingly audible chunter. Soon he was standing a few feet away. He was quite terrifying, actually, constructed from skin-clad sticks and an excessive quantity of black hair that sprawled around the receding chin of his inhuman face. Most striking was what I took, correctly I am now sure, to be his member. It called to mind a favourite page from the 1997 edition of the Guinness Book of World Records: 'The Man with the World's Longest Fingernails'. His thumb nail specifically: tightly coiled and brown, like a strawberry snail. It quickly became evident that the stick man was displeased by my presence in the pristine drifts of snow. 'Absolutely ruined!' he lamented. 'My perfect carpet of lilies! My lawn of diamonds!' I looked up at him with a lubricious smirk, attempting to toss my hair, although most of it remained stuck to my face. Emboldened by the blurry atmosphere of the dream, I asked, or rather, quipped, 'Got any Turkish delight?' It's hard to say whether he was angry. His eyes widened, his teeth clenched, and the great coil that hung between his legs twitched and flicked like the tongue of a snake. Then it unravelled completely and swung upwards like an incautiously operated crane. Unfurled and erect, it resembled a pole one might adorn with a severed head, or perhaps an artefact from the recurring dream of a trauma-tised veteran of the Vietnam War. There was a stringy drip of gunk hanging off the tip, and so, rather amusingly, it also took on the appearance of a fishing rod. Alongside his gnom-ish beard, I thought this rather fitting. My reactions were a little blunted in the prevailing conditions. It felt more like a lucid dream than any sober experience I could remember, however I was quite sure that this was one of those occasions upon which one ought to defend oneself. His part was so very narrow that I felt I could take it in two hands and bite into it like a Peperami, but this was not as easy as it looked. I grabbed hold of it with one hand and he immediately began to swing his pelvis from side to side, causing me to stagger back and forth a few times before falling heavily in the snow. The only other item I had in my possession was the vial with the black stuff at the end, and I had tucked this into the top pocket of my blouse. I appreciated that the thing showed little obvious potential as a weapon, but I had sensed the power of that dark gunk as I waited to access the disabled toilet. In one gloriously inspired moment, I once again seized his thrashing stick and quickly slid the tube over the end of it. The tip sank smoothly, deliciously into the black stuff. Steam rose amid a great hissing and fizzing, and as the creature sank weeping to his knees, I turned to address my swabbing hand: 'Where to now, my love?'

In the house across the road, I thought I could see the outline of the woman who lived there, standing behind the translucent blinds, observing me like a ghostly apparition. I smoked a cigarette before going inside

Coffee Tastes Better in Vietnam | Rob Brulee

At my parents' house there is a single framed photograph on the mantelpiece. The photograph is of me when I was a teenager. I am smiling at the camera, young red lips open wide, pink tongue round and soft just visible behind the front teeth of my lower jaw, and my eyes are the same colour as the bark on the trees in the woods behind my parents' house. I don't recognise those eyes now.

There are two things about this photograph that I find disquieting. The first is the eyes that look so unfamiliar and foreign to me—they are the same eyes I have now but I do not trust that they saw things in the way I see them now—and the second thing is that, at the corner of my mouth (you would only see this if you were to squint and hold the photograph an inch away from your face), there is a thin, pixelated smudge of dried blood that spreads to the left of my chin.

Until recently, I could not have said when the photo was taken or what had happened to the younger me to be posing like that, with a wide-open mouth and the blood stain by the lips, or why that photograph had been taken at all. The photograph had just become a part of the background of my parents' house and I paid it the same amount of attention that I would pay any other object they displayed, or the colour of their walls: I saw these things every time that I was there but I didn't notice them.

Last week, I was over at my parents' house checking up on my father after a brief stay in hospital due to his ongoing fight with the emphysema that resulted from a lifetime of smoking, when circumstance forced me to start noticing. My father was sat on the sofa watching a European football match on the television, shouting 'Vamos Los Blancos' occasionally to himself—even though he'd never been to Europe—and drinking from a dark bottle of beer. We had argued when I arrived, after I had got straight onto his case about now being the time to finally give up ('It's just a tickle on the lungs, nothing to concern yourself about'; he'd kept saying that line over and over again, 'Just a tickle on the lungs') and he had been largely ignoring me since. My mother was preparing supper in the kitchen and had implored me not to get him too excited so I scanned the living room, looking for something less provocative to talk about, and that's when I arrived at the photograph.

'When is that photo from?' I asked. The noise of the commentators' voices on the television was dull and tedious and I had to speak louder than I would have liked.

'What photo?' he replied, half paying attention, his focus still on the match.

'This one.' I took the photograph down from the mantelpiece and handed it to him, forcing him to properly notice.

Ah, that. That was the day you had your teeth removed. You were very happy with yourself and with what you were able to endure.'

I looked at him curiously. I had never had any teeth removed. I said this to him.

'Of course you did. When you were twelve years old. Three of them.' He coughed twice and kept his eyes on the television, moving forwards in his chair every time the small smudges of white surged towards goal.

'But why did I have them out?' I asked, trying to get his attention properly now.

'So they could fit your braces.' He looked at me with scrutiny. 'Well, you wouldn't remember having those, I suppose, as you wouldn't let them attach them to your teeth. You kicked up all manner of nonsense that day.'

He turned back to the television while I remained looking at him.

'You really don't remember? You can ask your mother if you don't believe me. Haven't you wondered what those great big gaps are in your mouth?'

I said nothing. Los Blancos scored and my father forgot all about our conversation.

My mother called us to dinner soon after and, while we ate, I kept my silence and noticed that I was having to remove food from between my teeth with more frequency than usual. Could it be that I had failed to notice something that was happening to me at an age when we notice things most of all? After dinner, as my parents sat drinking black coffee at the dining room table, I returned to the living room. I properly looked at the photograph for the first time and tried to

81

find something within the picture that I recognised: it was a portrait of me as young man, there must be something I could identify with, some way of stitching a thread between the image and the adult that looked at it. I searched through my memory for any hint of recognition about that day and that period of time but nothing came to me; I genuinely could remember nothing about it.

I returned home after that and mindlessly took the rubbish out to the bins at the top of the driveway. The houses next to mine were in darkness as they always were at that time of night. The only light in the street was the orange glow of the streetlamp, greasy with the early summer rain that had started to fall. In the house across the road, I thought I could see the outline of the woman who lived there, standing behind the translucent blinds, observing me like a ghostly apparition. I smoked a single cigarette before going back inside.

In bed, I thought about the evening and the conversation with my father. It was strange that I had asked my father about a photograph that I had never noticed in all the years it had been there on the mantelpiece; strange that I had entered my parents' house and immediately confronted my father—confrontation was something I usually shied away from. It was this incongruous approach that had led to my noticing of the photograph in the first place, which in turn had led him to recounting a story about me that I had no recollection of. Despite this, I mostly found it strange because

I had an appointment with my dentist the following day.

That night I dreamed that my father's teeth fell out.

The next afternoon, I left work early (I had been a teacher at the local secondary school for about four years) to make my appointment. It had been difficult to concentrate and my lessons were delivered half-heartedly and distractedly, and I was conscious that it was obvious that my mind was elsewhere. It is difficult to say whether this was due to the events of the previous evening, or the pervading sense of anxiety I always get when visiting the dentist. Perhaps I now knew why there was this underlying fear. I decided to ask the dentist about the forgotten tooth removal when I got there; as far as I could remember she had been my dentist my whole life.

There were many reasons why I disliked the dentist, even before the newly discovered tooth removal. I feared the probing metal instruments they would stick into my gums, the silicone gloved fingers that pulled at the sides of my mouth so carelessly that it felt like the corners would split at any moment, and I hated the feeling of the warm water that pooled in the back of my throat and splashed up on to my lips. There was also the taste of blood around the gums and on my tongue that didn't disappear for a couple of days. Whenever I was in the dentist's chair, it was impossible to focus on anything other than what was happening to me right then, in that moment. I could never take my mind elsewhere and I was hyperaware of every searching movement. There was also the greatest fear: that something would be wrong; that the dentist would find something and it would lead to further, more painful treatments. My pain threshold was intolerably low. And another issue had appeared the last time I had been there.

I had been sat in the waiting room, reading a book— perhaps a Garcia Marquez or a slim volume of Levy stories —and enjoying the sterile silence you only ever get in the waiting rooms of medical practices. Despite the uneasy feeling brought about by the concept of the dentist, there is something comforting about waiting when there is a defin- itive end point, and there was that afternoon. Reflexively, I would occasionally look up from my book to see if anything had changed—like a dog does when it has been sleeping, checking to ensure that all is as it was and it isn't missing out on anything—and generally the same stillness was present and I was the only patient. The young receptionist was the only other person there and she sat gazing into the distance, fiddling with her hair as she waited for the phone to ring and checking what I imagined to be incoming emails on a desktop computer. However, on one occasion when I glanced up, there was a figure moving at the far end of the corridor that was opposite where I was sat. It was a short corridor, with a door on each of the facing walls—the treatment rooms—and at the end of the corridor was a cupboard that I presumed contained medical supplies. Someone was going through this cupboard now. I could see their back and their arms, both covered in a blue gown, and it appeared that whatever they were looking for was costing them considerable exertion of energy as the posture and movements all looked laboured and uncertain. Someone who was new to their job and un-familiar with where things were in the cupboard, I thought.

This person turned around shortly after. I do not know how long I had been watching them but it felt like it had been some time—fixated, again, like the dog that has just awoken from sleep and has seen something is amiss. They made their way down the short corridor to the reception desk and whispered something in the ear of the young receptionist who seemed to not hear and made a gesture. The gowned figure removed the surgical mask from the bottom half of their face, and I instantly recognised the person beneath the mask.

It was a former student I had taught in my first year of teaching. A precocious young man with inky black hair and eyes like two round stones, which gave him an appearance of inner coldness, as if his subconscious were in a state of perpetual motion over what it was about to do. Most students are surprised to learn that their teachers barely think of them once they have left their care and this student was no exception. I don't think I had thought of him at all since he had left the school and I couldn't even recall his name then, which was perhaps a little odd as he hadn't been a normal student. Occasionally, perhaps once every two years, there are students that grow attached to the teaching staff and begin to view them as friends or relatives and try to remove the professional barriers. They linger at the end of lessons, listen to staff conversations for glimpses of personal information and then bring this up again at a future, removed date, like they are holding on to it, turning it over in their minds, thinking about when the worst moment to spring it would be. This was one such student. His attachment hadn't been to me but to female members of the department. But I clearly recognised him and knew he would remember me as I had often been there when he had stayed after school, sometimes up to an hour, in our small office, just hanging around and choosing not to go home.

Any moment now, I had thought, he is going to look up and he will notice me sitting here and then that will be it, he will not leave me alone and I will be at the mercy of his probing and prying lines of questioning. However, this is not what happened at all. He spent a lengthy period speaking in a hushed voice to the receptionist, not looking in my direction and he didn't look up and notice me when the receptionist received a call and announced that I could go into the dentist's room for my appointment. Even at the mention of my name, the former student didn't look up, just waited for the receptionist to finish and then went back to whispering in her ear.

It is difficult to say why this situation had unnerved me so much. I thought about it a lot after, certainly more than I had thought about the former student when he was at the school, when his behaviour was more alarming than it had been during that visit. His behaviour during the visit had been normal, and I think it was this that was bothering me. Whatever the reason, it had made me feel even more apprehensive about my visit to the dentist that afternoon. There was a heavy sense of dread sitting in my stomach that was attached to the former student, and it was growing larger as I got closer, as I walked down the endlessly straight road that led to the modest town centre and high street. If I had walked the other way out of work, taking a right rather than a left, I would eventually have arrived at home, although this required making a few turns and more presence of mind, but at least I would be further way from the dentist. This road was straight and long and the image of the dentist's surgery loomed heavy in the distance. Above me, the clouds were so dense that the sky was almost a milk white but there was a lingering heat and my shirt had started to stick to my chest, my armpits grew damp and my discomfort increased.

It was at this moment that I saw a car, still some way in the distance, veer across the road, so that it was driving along the wrong side of the carriageway but at speed and in my direction. It stopped right alongside me and the passenger door was flung open. A voice was trying to speak to me but I couldn't hear it over the noise of the engine, and I couldn't see the person the voice was attached to through the glare of the windscreen, so at that moment they were merely a ghostly apparition with a muffled voice. I had to manoeuvre myself around the open door, to the entrance and then bend down to see who it was and find out what they were saying to me.

'Would you like a lift home? I am heading that way. Would you like a lift?'

The voice that had spoken was a woman's and I looked her in the face now, a face that had something friendly but disconcerting to it. I didn't recognise the woman although there was something familiar about her. Her hair was dyed a bright blonde, the fringe straight and deliberate and her eyes were black and deep and watery.

'You don't recognise me, do you?' she asked. 'I live across

the road. I'm heading towards home so I can drop you off, if you like.'

In a film, or a work of literature, I would tell my students, we call this a *deus ex machina*. The moment when the protagonist is inconceivably rescued from danger by what can only be described as divine intervention (something my father was beyond, I might tell them, to add a personal touch). God interceding on the character's behalf in order to stop the narrative from being drawn to a premature close, or in order to ensure that there is a 'happy' ending and therefore the author or producer is able to make a wider allegorical point. Here was a woman I had never spoken to before, whom I knew existed but had never taken the time to notice, and she was offering me an escape from a potentially perilous situation. The appointment ahead had become a heavy burden (the former student, the missing teeth, the probing, the intrusion, the greater fear of what could be) and I accepted her offer. I did not think to ask her why she thought I was going home, considering I had been walking in the other direction and there is no route to get to the road that we both live on by walking the way that I was. But I accepted, grateful for the offer, too relieved to think about the strangeness of the situation and the circumstances, but buoyed by a genuine sense of elation.

I climbed into the car, my white shirt now stuck completely to my body, the coarse linen of my trousers uncomfortable against the sweat that had gathered on the hair of my legs. This state of discomfort quickly altered my feelings of relief as I realised that I would have to try to make conversation for the five-minute drive (perhaps longer due to an extensive stretch of road works that lined the main approach to our street).

The car moved away from the side of the road and she moved back to the right lane of the carriageway without looking in any of the mirrors. Silence on a car journey is something that you have to settle into and I didn't think that the journey would be long enough to get to that point, so that would mean forcing conversation substantial enough to fill the time. My neighbour (not really, but in a way) started to drum her fingers on the plastic casing of the steering wheel, readying herself to speak. The air in the car was close, almost stifling, and I noticed she had opted against turning the air-conditioning on. I sat and waited for her to speak and longed for the cool, artificial air.

'My son is in Vietnam, you know,' she started. 'Do you know where that is?'

I wasn't aware she had a son. I did know where Vietnam was and was prepared to answer. I'd been there twice. But she continued before I had the chance.

'It's a long strip of land that runs up the right flank of South East Asia. It is pretty much all coast. How fanciful is that? A country where the beach is so close, wherever you are. Even in the cities, you never have to venture too far to the sea and the sand is always bathed in golden light.'

She paused for a moment, wistfully thinking about the ocean and blue skies. We couldn't have been further from the sea at that moment. I undid the top button of my shirt, trying to manufacture some cool air, and waited to see if I should respond or if she would continue. The car moved steadily past the school where I worked.

'He rang me last night,' she continued, turning her head slightly towards me and taking her eyes off of the road. 'That was what I was doing when I saw you having a cigarette at the top of your driveway. We had been on the phone for about half an hour at that point and I like to take his calls in my bedroom, looking out at the street below, thinking about how different things are where I am. Last night, I could hear the waves crashing against the rocks in the distance, could almost feel the sand between my toes as I spoke to him. I waited all day for that call. It is funny what happens when you have children. Your life becomes all about them; you find yourself becoming of secondary importance. That's what's happened to me. My life is just waiting for him to call, to tell me things about his day or what he's been up to. The good and the bad. I want to hear it all. I would drink his words if I could.'

She had jumped off the edge and was moving into an area that was far too close and personal for how little we knew each other. Few people are capable of making acceptable, comfortable conversation with strangers. I was not one of them. I thought again about the former student with the eyes like two, smooth stones and how this situation would have been made for him. He had the required lack of shame.

We had arrived at the roadworks and the car slowed to a stop behind a red light.

'You know, he said the coffee in Vietnam is like nothing he's ever tasted before,' she said, the engine of the car throbbing, the heat drawing closer. 'It's so good, that he told me on the phone last week, that he would never drink coffee again if he came back home. It sounds like such a magical place, doesn't it? Imagine a place like that, where something is so life-affirming that you wouldn't touch it again in another place. He isn't just saying that as a tourist either. Even the locals drink it all day, every day. He said he met one woman who drank eight cups a day with two sugars in. Her teeth completely rotted away as a result but she still drinks the eight cups a day! Can you imagine a thing like that? An addiction so deep that you just keep doing it until it mutilates you? Perhaps the dental care isn't as good there. It would make sense.'

She stopped for a moment, the lines on her forehead deepening as she leaned back in her seat, taking both hands off of the wheel.

'It's funny really. Well, not funny, but strange, because of what happened to him after.' The light changed to green and she got ready to pull away. We were nearly at our road now. I thought about how I had barely uttered a word since I got into the car.

'What happened after?' I asked. She seemed surprised that I had spoken.

'The day after he had told me this on the phone, he was badly hurt, said he had got into an altercation at a bar in Hoi An, a small town that is, of course, on the coast. Three men beat him until he was bloody and raw, kicked him in the chest and the face, a real act of brutality. And it's odd that it was the day after he told me about the woman who drank so much coffee because he lost three teeth as a result, so that he now has three gaping holes in his mouth. It's awful. I just wanted to go to him, to look after him, cook a meal for him. He told me he was fine and not to bother, so I didn't. Just carried on waiting by the phone every evening for him to call. He seems okay now but I do worry about him.'

Now I knew she wasn't expecting a reply, I waited for her to continue as the car drew closer to the turning for our street.

'I could never read his eyes. I never knew what he was thinking, or what he might do next. Perhaps that has been the most difficult thing about him being away. What decisions is he making? I fear what is in him, fear what those uncommunicative eyes might do. He didn't tell me what led to him being so badly beaten. A random act of violence, he said, but I do wonder.'

She paused as she indicated to turn down our street.

'You met him once, you know.'

I had no recollection of this at all. The car was approaching our houses.

'Yes, once. He came to collect a package that was delivered to your address by mistake. Perhaps he is not so remarkable to look at, you might not have noticed his features. Beyond those dark, unreadable eyes, like two black pebbles, there is not much of note. He has dark hair and such strong, large hands. He is just like his father in that way. And that is another strange thing. Since he's been gone, I've started to imagine him, my son, in a different way. I have imagined him doing things that no mother should imagine her son doing. When we were on the phone last week, I could hear muffled laughter in the background, so high-pitched and unmistakeably female and do you know the only thing I could think about for the rest of the call? Those large, firm hands tightly gripping that girl's wrist. Holding on to her as he lay on top of her, her body writhing beneath his. Isn't that a strange thing for a mother to wonder of her son?'

The car pulled up outside our houses, parked at the edge of my driveway. She leaned over my lap and pulled a packet of cigarettes out of the glove compartment, took one out and lit it, inhaling deeply and holding on to the smoke.

'Children make you change,' she said and then exhaled the blue smoke from her nose.'Smoking, for example. That is something I'd never done before he left and then, one day, I decided to take the habit up and have smoked ever since. It's my favourite way to spend an evening: looking down at your driveway, blowing smoke into the summer evening air and waiting for him to call.'

She stopped speaking and sat silently, her lips taking greedy pulls from the cigarette, the engine humming around us. I opened the passenger door to let some air in and put one leg on to the pavement, making to leave. My neighbour undid her window an inch, flicked the remainder of the cigarette on to the road and then she looked at me.

'I'm wondering why you accepted my offer of a lift,' she said. I looked at her in surprise. 'It's just you were going the other way, so you can't have been heading home. I'm just wondering why you accepted. You don't need to answer. It's just curious.'

I left the car and shut the door, saw her take another cigarette from her packet, light it and start to pull away. Clearly she hadn't been heading home either. A thin column of smoke escaped from the window of the car as it turned a corner and sped away. The air had loosened, the clouds parting slightly to reveal thin strips of blue sky. There is a cherry blossom tree in the driveway of my home and the leaves were beginning to shed in the afternoon wind.

When I was inside, I stood and thought about the conversation for a while, not drawing any conclusions but allowing myself to be enveloped by a disquieting feeling while I observed how the light coming in through the windows in the kitchen illuminated all of the dirt and the dust and the crumbs. Afterwards, I called my parents' landline to check in on my father but nobody picked up so I left a message on the answering machine asking them to call back.

The rest of that day passed with nothing of note happening. I probably sat down to mark some papers, scribbling hard-to-read comments in the margins of students' work, probably made regular trips to the decking at the back of the house to smoke a cigarette and probably listened to a record by a band like Big Thief, one of their softer efforts as heavy music made me feel nauseous as I got older. I don't remember if my parents rang me back and I think I forgot all about the missed dental appointment; as far as I can recall, they didn't try and contact me. I struggle to recall exactly what I did that evening and, to be honest, the whole afternoon would have been forgotten if it hadn't been for what had happened this morning.

At around half past seven, I heard the letter box open and close, heralding the arrival of the morning's post. I had been sat at the kitchen table drinking tea and eating a breakfast of fried eggs and white toast and I moved towards the front door to collect the letters that had been delivered. At the top of the pile was a postcard. I didn't know anybody on holiday. On the front of the postcard was a familiar scene. A wide blue ocean—the kind of blue that doesn't feel real—filled the top half of the picture and dripped down into a bright white sand that made up the rest. In the top right corner was the beginning of an island formation and tiny smudges of black on the sand were probably sunbathers and tourists. In the bottom left corner was a flag I knew well, consisting of a red background and a bright yellow star right in the centre creating a migraine of colours. Across the top of the postcard in dark, cursive writing were just five words: Coffee Tastes Better in Vietnam. I turned the postcard over and knew what to expect. In childish script, she had written two short sentences: Let me know if you ever need a lift again. Come and find me anytime.

The afternoon came back to me like an unbiddable flood. Across the road, I could feel the presence of a ghostly apparition observing me from an upstairs window. Behind me, the landline began to ring and my stomach filled with hot dread.

I found a reference to him in Boswell's diary: a note about 'poor, mad Henry Gore, religious bookseller and poet, sent to Bedlam after molesting a poor girl'

Gore | Andrew Hart

I dream of Bedlam: the screams of the possessed and the insane, the brutality of the attendants and the stares of the curious. Amidst the noise and awful smells, the mockery and taunts, Gore wrote his chaotic poetry, his visions of the future and the strange love lyrics to his 'chosen'. Now he is slowly taking me over, bending me to his will, and there is nothing I can do about it.

It was in the basement of the library that I found the volume of poetry that would change my life: *The Wayfaring Spirit,* by Henry Gore. It was in the stack with all the other books that nobody reads. I loved spending my lunch breaks there, away from my colleagues: browsing and admiring the pictures in the antique atlases and illustrated novels. I luxuriated in the smell of leather from the old bindings and enjoyed the feeling that perhaps nobody had opened these pages for a hundred years or more.

From Putnam Green to Fulham
I hear the dying horses
Hear the souldered metal
—'Damnation'

There was not much in the way of biographical information in the book: just 'Henry Gore, Bookseller and Poet' and the date, 1736, on the title page; there was not even the name of the publisher. The pages were speckled with brown decay and were fragile—so much so that a couple had been half torn away. The volume contained some fifty-two poems, some little more than fragments, others much longer. Many were visions, or perhaps prophecies, some were descriptions of London, and there were romantic poems dedicated to an unnamed woman: his 'chosen'. The language was religious in tone, but straightforward and at times incredibly beautiful.

A collector from one of Harrogate's many second-hand bookshops had spent a day down in the stack before I began working at the library, He had bought anything of value and left the rest to moulder. Presumably, he'd looked at Gore's book, flicked through the pages, then put it aside. A volume by an eighteenth-century poet who was barely known even in his own time—what possible interest could that be? I suspect literary merit was not even a consideration. At least the library had not pulped it to make way for more computers or DVDs.

And why does he haunt me? His face on the frontispiece: unshaven beneath that wig, his dark, fervent eyes … as if he were trying to pass as respectable but could not help the darkness from his soul showing through. I scanned the portrait and stuck the enlarged copy on the wall facing my bed. I looked at him as I drifted off to sleep, or when Pete, my so-called boyfriend, came round to get his pleasure. Gore looked sternly down on me as he breathed in my ear 'Marie, fuck, fuck …'

> *My desire; blood and flesh, raven hearted*
> —'She'

The book lies on my shelf at home even today, after so much has been taken from me. The library would never notice it was missing as, according to the catalogue, nobody had ever borrowed it, and I doubt any of my colleagues knew of its existence. The red Harrogate Libraries binding, now faded, blended into my impressive eighteenth-century book collection; it was not the only volume that I had surreptitiously acquired over the couple of years that I worked at the library.

Why was the only published work of a poor London poet and bookseller who, as far as I know, never set foot in Yorkshire, found hidden in the basement of Harrogate Library? It should have been found in a London library, the city he wrote about. But none of them appeared to have a copy, not even the British Library. Perhaps this volume, stood on a shelf next to a biography of Alexander Cruden, was the only one left? And by chance after chance, ended up in my room.

I read the poems daily; in the morning, before setting off for work, and in the evenings, before I made my dinner, so that I knew many off by heart. I even read a couple of the easier ones to Pete whilst he waited to undress me and stick his thing in. But he just fiddled with his clothing and waited for me to finish so he could get on with the purpose of his visit.

And do you esteem me mad
Who serves the ravenous Lion
Who salves the bones of the poor?
—'Madness'

I went into a church one evening. A traditional-looking Anglican one, where they still used the *Book of Common Prayer* and where the congregation consisted of about thirty people, of whom I was, by some distance, the youngest. As I knelt in the pew, I prayed for Gore; prayed for him to come again and talk to me and be my friend. To create beauty out of dirt and squalor. To tell me to get rid of Pete who talks of 'Pakis and niggers' and yet who could be sensitive, at least until he'd cum inside me. And whom I could not bear to get rid of, because of the space in my life he would leave.

Mud, fæces and brown water
Where flyes and maggots breed
—'Ludgate Hill'

He was a middle-sized unobtrusive fellow, rather slovenly dressed for his class but otherwise unremarkable. But if you gazed into his eyes, you felt his melancholy and disqui- et. There was a musty smell about him, as if he had spent too long in the company of books, but his mind contained worlds of gods and devils, of the woman he sought and of a glorious future.

He was from the city and had never ventured far from its centre. Apprenticed to a bookseller as a boy, he eventually acquired enough money to buy his own bookshop in Chapman Street: a good location, right at the heart of things. He had been there ten years: a fixture in a city where things changed every day; where people died in the gutter and buildings fell apart.

And yet, although he was known as a bookseller, he regarded himself as a writer who sold books only to keep body and soul together. He wrote continually: poems, hymns and what he called 'outpourings', but they did not make him money, nor did they attract attention. His was a lonely life, without a servant or wife to tend to his needs. He was respected in the Presbyterian church he attended, despite his quietness and oddity, and by those who bought books from him, but he had no friends. Much of the time he was alone with his thoughts, which he wrote down, and which were more real to him than anything else.

Often he felt that he was just waiting: maybe for a sign, or for happiness. His parents were dead; his two sisters had not survived to womanhood. He was alone in the world, but whether this was a fate he had brought upon himself or one he had no choice over, he did not ponder. Nor did he bewail his fate; it was God's will and there must be a purpose behind it.

Gore's shop was small, dingy and dark, two doors away from the White Lion Inn. He specialised in theological works, particularly those of a Puritan view: *Baxter's Answer to*

Dr Stillingfleets' Charge of Separation, Diatribe, Discourses on Divers Texts by Joseph Mede, DD. *A Breviate of the Prelates' Intolerable Usurpations, etc* by William Prynne and *Annotations Upon The Five Bookes Of Moses, The Psalmes and the* Song of Songs, *or Canticles* by Henry Ainsworth. There were pamphlets of a similar type; *A Pastor's Secret Heart, The Sin of Man's Pleasing, Treason Against the Soul* and *Christ is All in All*.

He deplored the triviality of the age: the theatres, the music, the coffee shops. He imagined a return to the Protectorate of Oliver Cromwell, of blessed memory; of a true theocracy. Where was life going with this continual pursuit of pleasure? Even his fellow Presbyterians disappointed him, obsessed as they were with the everyday and the unimportant. And as for the clergy of the established church, he viewed them as emissaries of the devil, with their worldly ways and ostentatious dress. One day there would be a conflagration that would destroy all the wicked and bring in a new, most holy regime, a new Jerusalem, a light unto the gentiles.

She came into the shop: dark-haired and with eyes like a hawk. He knew that she was the One. She told him in her educated tones that her name was Rebecca. He did well not to clutch her to his heart. Hadn't he seen her arrival in his poem 'Bloodie Hearte', written after two days of prayer and fasting? She ordered a book for her father, a preacher at St Faith's, the church whose spire he could see from the doorway of his shop. He looked deep into her eyes, and for a moment she stared back, before withdrawing her gaze. But she knew; she could see. He undertook to bring her father's books to her house.

She haunts me behind the trees
A wraith or angel
—'Sweetness'

My flat felt like a prison. I waited for Pete to telephone or to visit without warning. It was a distorted relationship, based on our need rather than affection or even friendship. We used to work together in a supermarket before I got the job at the library. He is still there—deputy manager now, and likely to go places with his brash confidence. I was scared of him when we first met, particularly as he seemed fascinated by me, or perhaps saw me as somebody to conquer. But I was also attracted to his looks and charm, and his lack of worry about anything.

One day I was in the large freezer, making notes of what needed ordering, when he came down and stood close to me. And then we were kissing and I could feel him hard against me, and I pulled him closer, feeling wet and empty. I almost came as we thrust against each other; I quivered for a moment, not knowing where I was, but the feel of boxes of potato waffles against my bottom brought me to myself. That night he came to my flat and we finished what we had started.

We kept it quiet for a while, but then Pete told someone and soon everyone knew about our affair. I left soon afterwards to begin at the library. The relationship carried on, in a manner of speaking, but most of our communication was in the bedroom and we rarely went out, and on the few occasions we did, he never once held my hand. I knew that it was not any kind of love affair, but it was the closest

I could manage, and at least when my colleagues talked of their husbands and partners, I could mention Pete, so they realised that I was also loved and cherished.

Whilst I waited for Pete to call me, or ask me out somewhere, I tried to research Henry Gore. There was little or nothing on the internet, just the occasional mention of his bookshop in documents about London, and in directories, and I found nothing more about him in the library. I decided to go down to London for a couple of days and visit the British Library—it was about time I had a day out, and it would be an adventure of sorts. I didn't tell anyone where I was going, or why; not even Pete. I just went. I liked the sense that nobody knew where I was, even though they probably didn't care, or hadn't noticed, but I like to imagine I was cultivating an air of mystery.

I felt that my life was insubstantial, close to being torn aside and if it was, what would be left? Someone writing feverishly by candlelight, with almost illegible handwriting, struggling to keep the world together?

Emptiness, trees asunder, where is my God?
—'Solitary'

Rebecca was on her own when Gore came to her father's house. She let him in and he delivered the parcel into her hands. He bent over her and kissed her hard, and as her mouth opened he bit her tongue, and tasted her blood. His hands touched her breasts, and he squeezed them hard, and she muttered something and dropped the books. He looked directly at her as he held her, and then he left. He had not said a word. That night he wrote, never stopping until the day broke and it was time to open his shop. His room smelled musty, of unwashed flesh and of tallow from the candles that he'd burnt.

He thought of her as he sat in his shop that day. It was a hot summer, and the smell of the busy streets came into his shop: horse and human shit, sweat, meat and unnameable odours. He could still taste on her on his lips and feel her body pressed against him; her bosom, large and uncontained in his hands.

For so long he had imagined a woman who would share his labours and to be his companion in all things. But the few women he met seemed unworthy, or scared of him. He never stopped believing God would provide a helpmate for him, it was just a matter of being patient, of waiting for the right one. There was so much of marriage in the *Bible*, and it was not good for man to be alone. Perhaps all this was a prelude to a better life.

Some time after midday, three men walked in and, without a word, carried him off. One was Rebecca's father, the minister, and the other two were large men, servants or roughs hired for the occasion. They carried him away into a carriage. He was calm at first, thinking they were taking him to Rebecca, but as the carriage carried on and on, he realised they were taking him farther away. He kicked at the walls and tried to call for help, but the two roughs jumped on him and held him down. The rest of the journey was spent on the floor with a boot jabbed into his guts and the smell of sweat and garlic engulfing him. He wept softly, imagining Rebecca longing for him and wondering why he hadn't come.

I walked the streets he had walked, wondering how they had changed since he had lived there. All the people thronging the streets, so many of them, and the noise of buses and cars—and what would he make of the Tube? Then there are the tall buildings of metal and glass, reflecting the glaring July sunshine, that I found intimidating. Surely if Gore were transported forward in time, he would go mad? Crawl in a corner and start to shake, hoping that it would all go away.

Even the British Library was modern, with its online catalogue and plenty of laptops on display. But unfortunately there was little on Gore: just a few more references from contemporaries—but it was his 'Presbyterian' or 'Puritan' bookshop, not his poetry, that was mentioned. I wondered how many people had actually read his writing, or whether I was the only one?

But then, by chance, I found a short reference to him in Boswell's diary: a note about 'poor, mad Henry Gore, religious bookseller and poet, who was sent to Bedlam after molesting a poor girl.' Was this the same person? I knew that it must be, and whilst elated that I'd found something more about him, I was horrified. Molested? What did that exactly mean? Beneath that wig and his religion, was he just a dirty old man?

There was certainly an air of madness about the poems, but could this be true? Did he die in that asylum, friendless and mad? Were his poems just the ravings of a Bedlamite? Someone who deserved to be in prison after blighting some poor innocent's life? But although he seemed to be looking for love, there was little sex in his poetry, and even that was vague and ambiguous. He did not fit the cliché of the prurient Puritan.

Apparently, there were no records for Bedlam for that date; people were sent there, and disappeared. Not like now, when everything we do causes a record to be printed and a form to be filled. Despite annoying librarians, I could not find out what had happened to him afterwards, nor how long he was incarcerated and whether he had died in Bedlam or somewhere else. There was nothing more to be found. None of the London parish registers mentioned him, apart from one possible baptism.

> *The stench of us*
> *Even in God's holy house*
> *It beats the wind*
> *And engulfs*
> —'Enclosed'

After spending most of the day in the British Library, I tried to find where he had lived. The only place I knew associated with him was his bookshop on Chapman Street, which I discovered was now called Evelyn Street, not far from St Paul's. There were no street numbers in those days, but apparently it was two doors along from the White Lion Inn. I surreptitiously photocopied a trade directory and an old map of roughly the correct date so that I could work out where the bookshop had been.

I soon found the road. Suited men and women walked along it looking busy and important and unaffected by the hot sun on their backs; it was late afternoon and they were probably going home after a hard day making money. There were the headquarters of several banks, some offices and a modern pub with some silly name that advertised football. I wondered if this were the site of the White Lion. The street had changed so much from when the map was drawn that I couldn't be sure, and I had no idea where the bookshop would have been. I stayed there for an hour, but just couldn't make the map and the present correspond. I felt nothing of Henry's spirit in this street, dedicated to the capitalist way and to mindless pleasure.

I felt heard a footstep behind me, briefly and then it was gone. I had no idea why I noticed it when there was so much noise, and so many footfalls about. And then I felt a presence, or maybe just a smell: not scary, but something from another time: archaic and damp, like the odour of old books. It hit me for a moment and gradually faded. Then everything was back to normal, and I moved aside to avoid a young man talking earnestly on his mobile phone.

I could see a church spire through a cluster of buildings, so I made my way towards it. I entered the building and sat there for a while. The church was called St Faith's and—according to a leaflet I bought for a pound—there had been a church on the site since before Gore's time. It looked pretty modern to me: certainly, the pews and windows were not as Gore would have seen them, although the building itself was much older. Perhaps this had been the church he had attended. I sat there trying to get a feel of him, find a bridge between us, and for a few moments I felt some peace.

There was a bookshop at the back of the church. I looked at the books and bought a CD of anthems by Henry Purcell.

As I waited to pay, I caught a whiff of that damp smell again. It might have been coming from a tramp trying find somewhere out of the heat of the late afternoon, but I couldn't see anyone. I then found my way back to my hotel and had a shower.

That night I walked the streets of the West End, just out of curiosity, and with no particular end in sight. Gradually, I became conscious that there were footsteps behind me, steady but not loud, and there was that smell again; not overpowering, but definitely there. I wasn't scared, just curious and puzzled, as if it were taking place in a book I was reading. I stopped and looked at a poster for a revival of *My Fair Lady*, and the footsteps stopped too. I swiftly turned around, but there was nobody there, or perhaps a shadow that faded when I gazed at it. I continued walking, and felt a breath on the back of my head—just a quick puff, that was all. And as I made my way back to the hotel, I could still hear the footsteps: quiet but persistent.

Throughout the rest of Marie's stay in London, she felt somebody at her shoulder: disapproving, cross, yet curious as to the things she was looking at. The footsteps also continued; at times she forgot about them, but then in a moment of silence she would become aware again. And that damp smell became a part of her, so that she became immune to it. Even on the train back to Leeds she felt there was somebody behind her. She hoped that once back in Harrogate, the presence would disappear—but this did not happen. That spirit was always at her shoulder, and the footsteps a step or two behind; quiet but solid.

A moonlight shadow, fleeting then gone
Oh Lord, is this my faith?
—'Trust'

That night Pete came round; his very presence disgusted her.

'I missed you,' he said, and sniffed.

'Did you? What did you miss?'

'This,' he replied with a laugh and started to kiss her.

She disengaged herself. 'Is that it? Someone just to fuck?'

He shrugged. 'What is wrong with that? You enjoy it too,' he said. 'More than I do.'

She slapped his face and he glowered at her before departing.

She looked at herself in her mirror, rearranged herself and put on the disc of anthems by Henry Purcell she had bought at the church in London.

'Remember not, Lord, our offences, Nor th' offences of our forefathers. Neither take thou vengeance of our sins, but spare us, good Lord.'

'Spare me,' she thought. 'Spare me and make me whole.'

At work the following morning she felt dissatisfied with everything; all around her was trivia and nonsense. Is this all she wanted? She was not close to her colleagues at the library, but she got on with them well enough, and enjoyed hearing about their lives. They were all a little older than her and all were married with children, which made them seem even more so. But since getting back from London, it all seemed so endlessly pathetic and unimportant; talking about television, their nights out, their holidays, their awful children …

One evening she got home and turned on her television, but it was loud and bright and just rubbish. Even shows she used to enjoy seem vapid and unimportant. She switched it off and glared at it as it sat in the corner. Eventually, she unplugged it, picked it up and, staggering slightly, took it downstairs and put it in the large skip that had been in the front yard of the flats since she had moved in. Perhaps she could have given it to somebody, but why would anybody have a use for such a thing? Marie put on Radio Three and an organ concerto by Handel played as she read another poem by Henry Gore.

Sweet swirling colours
I saw you drift towards me o'er the green
—Untitled

He could afford a private cell and was given food and also paper and pen so he could write. He soon was settled in and did not fret; he even forgot about Rebecca, trusting that he would find her sooner or later, or that she would find him. He had been diagnosed with 'religious melancholia' by James Monro, the asylum's physician, and as a consequence was bled once a day, but otherwise left alone. In many ways he was as happy here as he was in his bookshop, being oblivious to his surroundings, the noise and the smell. His thoughts were always more important than what he did and where he was.

He stayed in Bedlam for a month, before some acquaintances of his—a minister from his church and two Presbyterian businessmen—brought him out and promised to look after him. The Rev Thomas Swaney offered to let him stay in his house but Gore declined.

'I am not mad, just a little disturbed; I need to get back to my shop and to my poetry.'

And so they allowed him to do that. He looked dishevelled and ill, sat in the dimly lit shop reading a Bible, almost stifled by the smell of the tallow candle. He missed the asylum, where he had been safe from well-wishers from his church and the customers who were forever popping in and trying to buy things.

Sometimes I walked about the streets, and went past the house where Rebecca lived. I was tempted to knock and beg admittance; speak to Rebecca or even her father. I knew that if I could be allowed to talk, then I could explain things. But perhaps Rebecca was from the devil, sent to tempt me from my work of writing. I needed to stop relying on impulse; the forces of evil were more far more cunning than I.

I dozed as I read, and heard many sounds; endless people walking, horns, vehicles. There were fantastical buildings made of glass and strange materials that rose oppressively up and made me gasp from dizziness. I swooned for a moment, but then was woken by someone coming into my shop, and they talked to me for a while, and then they left. But in my head, all I could see was that city, and all those people, and all that wealth, that glass. At first I thought it was London in the future, or some other great city, but then I realised that it must be Heaven, the golden city filled with golden people, all marching out to do good and to help their brethren. As was natural to me I wrote down what I had seen, praying as I did so, and thanking God for such a vision.

> *A Star was Glowing on this stormy night*
> *People beating with wings, with light*
> —'A Vision'

Marie started to attend churches, sometimes three on the same Sunday. On occasion she would see people who visited the library, but she avoided talking to them. Indeed, she rarely spoke to the congregations or even the vicars or ministers, hurrying away as soon as the service had finished, or even before. She went to a Mormon church for several weeks, attracted by the austerity and guilt that seemed a fundamental part of their religion, but found the ridiculousness of their creed overwhelming. When they started pressuring her into being baptised she stopped going and forgot about them.

She continued with her job, but it passed in a blur.

'Are you okay, Marie?' asked her manager, Jane. 'You seem awfully distracted. Have you got something on your mind? Have you fallen out with that boyfriend of yours?'

She struggled for a moment to remember who that was.

'Henry? Oh, you mean Pete. No, that's been over for weeks—since I came back from London. I'm just a bit tired. Perhaps I need a change.'

'Are you thinking of leaving?' wondered Jane. 'We'd be sorry to lose you.'

'No, no,' Marie muttered, and walked off.

'She's a strange woman,' thought Jane, and realised she knew very little about her. Even Pete was just the name of someone whom most of Marie's colleagues didn't believe existed.

Marie did leave, but not by choice. She had always stolen the odd book: 'liberating', as she saw it, volumes that were stuck in the basement and never borrowed. She would take them home and delete them from the catalogue, so it was as if they had never existed. But now she started taking books from the main library: ones she disliked and disagreed with, mostly about film stars or populist religions, and what she regarded as chick lit. She would rip them up and put them in her recycling bin. The more time went on, the more books she found she disliked. Even the latest Booker Prize winner did not pass muster. She found it silly and superficial, so she destroyed it, too.

So long as she stuck to the occasional obscure book, Marie might well have remained undetected, or even been tacitly encouraged. But she got more and more blasé about her thieving, and when she was found carrying a bag full of books out of the building, Jane did some detective work, and Marie was dismissed the following morning. She emptied her locker in silence and left the building, darkness buzzing inside her head, the footsteps following her home, sounding stronger today.

The police came around and searched her flat. They took away most of the books she had purloined from the library; fortunately she had hidden the volume of Gore's poems and a couple of others that were precious to her. The two policemen, polite and apologetic, did not search very thoroughly.

The council took her to court over the missing books, and she even appeared on the front page of *The Yorkshire Post*; her case was not helped by her dishevelled appearance when she appeared in the dock, nor the accusations of anti-intellectualism and blasphemy that she levelled at the North Yorkshire library service. She was fined and eventually paid up, as she could not even face the thought of prison. She was humiliated, and over the next few weeks often woke up aghast at how she had destroyed her life. It was true that it had not been great before, but it had at least seemed secure. Now she was falling into a pit of chaos.

Her sister in Basingstoke offered her a room, but Marie refused, preferring to stay in Harrogate. It was her home, after all. She did voluntary work in an animal shelter three days a week. The other volunteers tended to leave her alone, or perhaps Marie left them alone, preferring to talk to animals and keep her thoughts to herself.

In her spare time, she tried to write a biography of Gore; she worked on it for five years, but as she did not have enough information, it was all guess work and fantasy. She turned it into a novel, but with no more success. She then wrote to publishers with copies of his poems, in the hope that one would bring out a volume of his work. A couple did show interest, but nothing became of it. Eventually, Marie gave up, although Gore remained the only man in her life, that life became a slow decline; she remained alone and friendless.

A rich man from Yorkshire, one Henry Greene, a member of our faith came to see me. I had not been well, laid up in bed and just getting up to write my visions and other phantasmagorical stuff. My shop had remained closed and I did not miss the customers, the smells and the dust … especially the dust. And there were always voices and footsteps.

I sold up, and Greene took me away with him to live with his wife and children in a large house a little outside the spa town of Harrogate. He had an extensive library and he wanted me to organise it; but there was no rush, and he fed and clothed me very generously, leaving me with no wants or needs. He allowed me to eat with his family, but I usually preferred to dine alone and when I wanted. I realised he was being kind, but he could afford it and I worked hard for my money, putting his books in order and creating a thorough catalogue.

It is a modern house but lovely in an ordered sort of way, with gardens, and in the distance there are fields with sheep, a bleakness I love. I hope that I never have to leave here. A few miles away there is a ruined abbey, and often I walk there, and sit and pray, engulfed by the beauty of God's world, before I have to return to humanity.

And of course I have plenty of time to write. Sometimes I think that I am truly insane with what comes out of my head, but I know that the world is a very strange place and that the devil walks about handily. And writing helps me to get a grip on it all, to keep my world together and to keep it stable.

Towering darkness
Sheep who bleat in melancholy
Oh, what is this?
—'Pastoral Scene'

And this girl who haunts me: Marie. I write down what I know of her, and give her life; and I feel her heartbreak and loneliness far away and beyond my reach. I see her world that I have created: a very different England. My heart breaks for her, even though she is just a phantom of my own conjuring. I just wish I could write her a happy ending; bring her peace and love. Especially love.

Abandoned, snivelling wee Aleister was left to traipse unsupervised around the well-stocked mall, pressing against the glass exteriors of mixed-brand department stores, fashionable clothing boutiques, electrical retailers, on-trend accessory vendors and luxury goods emporiums hosting award-winning Provençal face cream concessions

Psychoneuroses | Evan Hay

Slouched beneath yon immense, lonely ash tree, grooving to Yiddish-related acidic house, he greedily interfered with a lap-dancing Norn. Pungent little sort it was: halitosis, thick Irish accent, decked out in crotchless knick-knocks, peephole bra, and dishing out plenty of extreme close-up. Bending over backwards it was, chomping his knob raw yet falling asleep prior to eruption. She couldn't even be arsed to spit out a prophecy (other than mumbling that Aleister's skimpy future had been sold by declension monkeys, on the orders of the universal grinder). What a tease. In revenge, wearing a raincoat on his pecker, he shunted her up her fibrous butt like a jackhammer. Oh, it was gripping all right; just a pity an amalgam of dour fate and high anxiety decreed Aleister never would get to blow his Old English. Up jumped a troll from under a humongous fungus, soliloquising ten-to-the-dozen. She clocked Aleister and threw a wobbler. 'It's all over, son; you've blown it. Rustication time.'

It was all kicking-off that summer. In the wake of public spending cuts, BA helicopters plunging into the Celtic
sea, temperatures soaring, the Old Queen's Guard wilted
under bearskins ... And still, it wasn't nearly as perfervid
as the previous, when Goose Green and racially aggravated
consumer riots set the scene for a hair-raising intrusion
into monarchical mystique. Enter Mickey Fagan, Aleister's
old schoolmate, transmogrified, a tad unexpectedly, from
sardonic gamin into star struck palace prowler. Aleister
was loath to jump to conclusions, yet recursively suspect
to his circumspect reasoning was that, national notoriety
notwithstanding, Fagan's alleged torch crimes and ostensible
double trespass carried no legitimate conviction. Despite
fractals of quasi-journalistic investigation, no one appeared
able or willing to corroborate any intelligible brass tacks.
Each pejorative exposition differed in crucial details from
its manufactured predecessor, resulting in fabulations, mis-
carriages of justice, and a palpable economy with the truth.
Nevertheless, Fagan, the stock-in-trade madman, had exited
stage left, to be housed at Her Majesty's sarcastic pleasure.

Aleister himself acquired insights into shenanigans behind
the story months before its cognate scandal belched, having
sampled the fellowship of Fagan and a gang of the saga's key
players on a night out to celebrate the absolving conclusions
reached in Lord Cyprian's report (formulated to close the
book on a Security Commission inquiry). It was a jolly, on
expenses, courtesy of some big knob from Royal Protection

codenamed Trestle-Table: a group commander who, in con-
junction with his deluxe entertainments budget, could afford
to support sordid and degraded company. Amusingly, the
copper's favourite bed-hopper tagged along: a hustler called
Roach, who tittered nervously and kept holding hands with
his philanthropic squeeze; he alluded to the senior officer
as 'my Vicky Order nut gone commando'. This subversive
posse, all lovely boys together, cruised (with some random
wandervögel from the Canaries thrown in for good measure)
from that well-appointed political nexus of Highbury Fields
to rip it up, binge drinking around N1. Aleister's remembrance was frayed (same world, different planet). What was
certain was he'd gotten shickered, and grown inexorably
attracted to the witty Spaniard. By the time they alighted
at The Famous Cock, Aleister had lost it completely: quiz-
zing the young caballero in an ill-defined monologue that
over-indexed Norwich City Football Club. Amid a dense
cloud of king-size cigarette smoke and acute embarrassment,
with the help of pictures mapped onto scraps of paper, it
was comprehensively pointed out that he'd sorely misunderstood the Guanche guy's allegiances: Pedro wasn't the
least bit interested in association football. But then, neither
was Aleister. He went for a leak, recovering his composure
before returning to the fray, which was heady fare by anyone's standards: commentaries on political stasis, corruption
and dire warnings that Britain's population would soon be
consigned unto a neo-Dark Age: an upcoming epoch her-
alded by societal crises (a series of vicious events, which
Trestle-Table delighted in referring to as 'the Doctor Marten's
apocalypse'). By this juncture, Aleister had heard enough

121

seditious gossip to develop an unhealthy appetite for com-
plots, chiefly state-endorsed crimes against the proletariat.
Despite that, on account of his unrequited love affair with
loss and sorrow, he felt vulnerably ineffectual. Daring to
fight the powers-that-be was unimaginable. Even in dreams,
he couldn't escape the aching disappointment of coexisting
with negative expectations; self-critically, he'd grown aware
that he was the sort of frenetic, psychometrically tested,
unfit-for-purpose loser who'd naus up a civil protest big style.

Fagan's wasted youth (sympathetically understood in the
context of psychological praxis) harboured a passion for
zestful revolutionaries cum urban guerrilla types, especially
those prepared to go the full nine anarchic yards. Mickey
was fascinated by social inequity, royal prerogative and class
war, positing (after sedulous consideration): who the flipping
hell wouldn't rebel? By way of contrast, Aleister had experienced little enough welfare from trickle-down economics, his
neighbourhood, or his estranged parents (galling little-or-no
hopers scunnered by a lifetime's penury). During reception
year, on the eve of sports day, his depraved bearded father
(*damnation memoriæ*) buggered off, and whilst mother dear-
est kept social workers at bay, there was precious little time
left between her two cleaning jobs and recurrent *affaires de
cœur*, for mother–son levity. Unsurprisingly, he'd never felt
loved or wanted; more like some dusty ornament- a token
curio from an ephemeral union. Aleister could only aspire to
the warm devotion extant between Fagan and his diminutive

twinsetted mater. Their cradle-to-grave relationship wasn't flagrantly unconventional, yet Aleister sensed an intense, abnormal, selcouth aura: a kind of primitive joy. *À bon entendeur, salut*: Aleister and Fagan's mutual, ginger Piggy O'Brien (panel beater by profession, farceur by vocation), the grinning, stertorous, no-nonsense pragmatist of their thirty-something, Anglo-Hibernian clan of three, curtly trashed such unguarded speculation as 'utter bollox', counselling Aleister to keep shtum, or face extreme consequences. Quick with fists and temper, violent and territorial, Fagan smack-battered his pink stepdads purple. Eschewing happy family idealism (Piggy viewed Fagan's domestic straighteners as expressions of a natural will to power) Piggy maintained council estate heritages weren't wealthy enough for such dispensable romanticism, gloomily contending airy-fairy fancies manifestly aren't entailments of unprivileged lifestyles. Be that as it may, O'Brien's bog-hopper parents did stick with the sanctity of marriage, if only to celebrate a silver jubilee. Theirs was an elegantly understated party, gay beyond belief: Joe Loss and his Orchestra played over the gramophone, cocktails and vol-au-vents were served upon crepuscular rays of midsummer sunlight to underwhelmed public bar acquaintances, and a few pasty faces from their 1930s terrace. Pigsty's nonchalance was typical of someone who had always enjoyed the love and commitment of an adhesive family; he simply took it for granted. Aleister cried a river; Fagan danced a well rehearsed tango with his old lady, and gin slings washed the shores of dawn.

After Mrs Fagan died, her singleton son grew increasingly obsessed by the notion of a wholly exposed, crudely infibulated woman as head of state; it agitated and aroused him in equal measure. What otiose limp-wristed protection was afforded Her Majesty by the tightly-wrapped prince regent? Fagan ceremoniously placed QE2 on the same lofty pedestal as his own mother; a trophy for vile men, offering little or no emotional support to their booty. Mickey envisaged Elizabeth Regina forcefully fist-fingered, before being mounted posteriorly and sausaged Greek style; crass libidinous fantasies deranged whatever particles of sense remained, rendering him unsure whether to fuck or fight his Glücksburgian adversary. An incorrigible romantic, when push came to shove, inspired by Ken Russell's audacious *Women in Love*, Fagan settled on stripping-off for a tipsy bout of Japanese-style wrestling, amid the firelight of the Duke of Dunedin's bedchamber. The nationals reported that Fagan was gallantly tackled by dapper footman Phil McCavity (since retired), a queer chap who was oddly reticent concerning his personal involvement in the drama. London Lighthouse carers insisted that McCavity wouldn't say boo to a goose. Fagan would, though: hissing loudly down Camden Passage market on behalf of antiquarian operations, many of whose traders were enamoured by the cut of his jib. It was a ragtag and bobtail cash-in-hand confederation, but he'd been earning a few quid at the time so it was right mauve him to rock the sloop, what with three million unemployed. Directly preceding his iconic faux pas, Fagan had inadvertently violated an Islington council byelaw. Tipped-off, housing association policy and procedure staff complained about his grunting pet (it transgressed his tenancy agreement); Fagan swore blind he didn't harbour one, although a particularly cynical girl-next-door insisted she investigate. Behold! No fish or fowl, while Mickey, without a trace of embarrassment, boasted that the theriomorphic-like din resulted from his beasting a string of high-maintenance erotopathic lovers. Not one to be duped, Fagan's nosey neighbour insisted she put his explanation to the test: *hic Rhodus, hic salta* (or vernacular sundries to this effect). So Mickey, howling like mad, banged her doggy-style so hard he got a ruddy nosebleed and earned himself the sobriquet 'Rudolph'. Still unsatisfied, the dopey tart opted to sue him for noise pollution via the borough's pro-feminist social compliance unit.

'Bloody hell, ma'am, what's he doing 'ere?' A shrill alarm was sent ringing round the City of Westminster by HRH's flummoxed chambermaid, given the screaming abdabs by Mickey, supposedly supping from a carafe of half-inched Californian Riesling. How exciting! Let's face it: Fagan was in no fit state to endure the resulting ordeal. That very morning he'd been involved in a heart-rending squabble over the ownership of a cut-and-shut motor, aspirated a leaded lungful of mouth-siphoned four-star, and for reasons best known to himself, was masquerading as Rudolf Hess. Upon popping into his local barbers in Finsbury Park (for a short-back-and-sides), Fagan announced he was tidying himself up ahead of a prestigious tiffin appointment with His Grace the Duke of Hamilton & Lady Nina, over which they were scheduled to address miscellaneous thorny issues revolving around the duchess' campaigns for animal rights. No sober assessment of his condition would have judged him capable of scaling spiky railings, burglar-proof drainpipes, nor leaping roof-to-roof like an orang-utan. Tell me, just how did Fagan elude Buck House's 24/7 security? And what precisely defined his shady, sadomasochistic relationship with wrinkly Prince Philip, whose bruised sphincter, rumour had it, was treated by that venal, royally beknighted arse specialist Dr David Croft: famed purveyor of platinum ring-holes, for celebrity coke addicts. In a futuristic John DeLorean world of cocaine cosmetics, monogrammed DDC rectal accessories were the last word in reassurance for syringe users, aiming to keep bugles clean, and septa intact. Word-on-the-street was, the grand old duke had been cornholed and felched until his puce tuchus resembled the Jack and Danny of a Guinea-Bissau baboon. Of course, it was a cover up- although Fagan confessed to several prison psychiatrists that he'd tasted better genitals. Whisper from that whatever tenuous conclusions you fancy. The Old Bailey beak certainly did.

Instanter, Aleister realised he was alit, retrograde; having been tossed on the serrated horns of a dilemma, before plummeting from the upper levels of a multi-storeyed identity crisis. Gasping for air in front of London Underground's bleak LIFT OUT OF SERVICE sign, Aleister feared losing his will to live within an admonitory pit of despair at Goodge Street tube-station. Stone me, another bloody *trou-de-loup*!

Mortal peril was too close for comfort; somewhere along life's impermanent way he'd taken a wrong turn. Festooned by beads of oily sweat, Aleister ascended a one hundred and thirty-nine-step staircase to egress, stood outside the building's oxblood red faïence blocks, palpitating, and timorously suffering all manner of oesophageal reflux, he rolled a fat liquorice paper fag while trying to gauge the extent of this most up-to-the-minute mental lapse. Still tripping, he clocked a CCTV system overhead and so, in a public display of proleptic irony, pretended to be in complete control of internal impulses and external traumas. Meandering awhile, muttering scurrilously, before heading off down Berners Street to those mawkishly bathetic Ancienne Forge tearooms on Berwick Street. Paul Raymond's mock Vichy venue's architectural splendour provided a makeshift video recording studio; its art deco interior offered scant pain relief from an excruciatingly naff fare of trademarked light entertainment spotlighting burlesque French missionaries clumsily shriving, whilst pursuing comic strip crusades against adult themed revues that the Grand Order of Water Rats officially pooh-poohed as misogynistic pornography. A clientèle chic of playboy property developers were treated to a caricaturish cast, bursting at their nylon seams with apotropaic mumbo jumbo as they brokered a mesmerising repertoire of life insurance options (bons marchés as far as Aleister could tell), plus slapstick servings of featherweight double entendres across disposable platters. A troupe of superficially wanton, but distinctly naïve mini-skirted waitresses sported black patent stilettos, tantalising hi-vis stocking tops, with sun-ripened honeydew melons squeezed into sheer, plunge-cut white silk blouses. All in their early twenties, these heartbreakers passionately vied for Equity cards by advertising a synthetic 'take-me-from-behind' coquetry. *Bien sûr*, for the sake of flickering proprieties, they also served luxurious leaf teas in fine bone china mugs.

'*Une tasse de bohea, s'il vous plaît mam'zelle.*'

Furtively checking his bins, Aleister felt relieved to grope a plenitude of coins of the realm, a travel-card for zones one-to-three, two well-worn ribbed condoms, a small cuneiform clay tablet, plus friable early-door midweek comps for Madame JoJo's, from whence hallucinogenic drugs and maladaptive daydreaming had instigated that impromptu mission to Yggdrasil (a right schlep on the Northern line). Occult Hindi messages garbled from the driver's cab terminated his zero-hour tube journey in Mornington Crescent; bewitched, he'd popped out for an eyelash, but spent an unheralded Thursday night frottaging with that swarthy trog from County Kilburn. Sweet Jesus! He'd monster-snogged mad Paddy's emphysemic missus, two-bob Aoife, numerous times. Hot ruddied tongues inside rasping mouths, smooching and slavering; culminating in ultra-smelly staccato sex with both their zippers closed. He hadn't climaxed mind, so he'd probably be okay. Psych! He lit a joint; even as a resting actor he figured it was outrageous, juxtaposing sensuously alluring gusset with Christianity. Bearing his order, a leggy, pussy-pelmetted factotum enquired after the state of his soul: inferno, purgatory, or paradise? You're having a laugh! Ogling the ample cleavages on display, one in particular caught his attention: her nametag read Brigitte. *Oh là là*. Was she a Bertie? Doubt it. Dear Brigitte, give us a wank.

'You 'ave not come to see ze peeping show I 'ope?'

Brigitte smiled ear-to-ear as her sultry French accent triggering an amatory frisson that stirred Aleister loins. Momentarily intimidated, he rose to leave without tipping, laughing off her dolorous suspicions that he was tuned into Betamaxes showcasing girls on the run from Oldham social services. On the hoof, Aleister nonchalantly cased the joint, wandering past replica nudes (including Auguste Rodin's *Le Baiser*), and a grandiose art nouveau mirror. He cast a bitchy moue at his faltering baroque reflection- begging the question: did he resemble an unbalanced pervert? If so, he'd best buy a pick-me-up. Aleister did not dare appear unhinged or worse (creepy) in Heaven- his aspirational destination. There geezers camped themselves up a class, for competition was bristly stiff inside that grand celestial residence, where a kiss without a moustache was like an egg without salt. Yuk!

Aleister decided to procure something special to slip into mademoiselle's café latte, in the course of a future assignation. Opportunely, Piggy was due live on stage at the Divine Comedy Store's Friday matinee; he was odds-on to hold a few banging party tricks up his ropey sleeve- enough to loosen Brigitte's resolve. K-I-D, mum's the word. Shame Aleister needed to date-rape her, as he didn't consider himself a misogynist. In fact, he liked ladies well enough; not the wicked ones who found him wanting, but he and balked at latent notions of punishing, hurting, or damaging them. That said, he failed to see women as equals, soul sisters, or trustworthy friends. Through his grimy doors of perception, the second sex represented objects of desire: dolly birds, some of whom he'd been able to train up & domineer for while. Brigitte possessed several serviceable aspects sweet enough to buoy his horribly warped tri-sexual mind. If only she could button her quivering lip, and turn an amenably blind eye to his eccentric affairs of the flesh, he may even propose to her: anything to leave a lump in her throat. Strolling along Gerrard Street chewing a chunk of Peking duck, he formally decided that he could never endure monogamy on account of his innate needs for bimbos, priapic saunas, peppercorn rent boys, Qabalistic weekends, ritualistic blood-drinking sessions and other hobbies essential for a relaxed middle age. But young Brigitte, despite her femme fatale façade, was, in Aleister's estimation, prim and proper. Add assertive female to practising Roman Catholic, teetotaller or, (God forbid) virgin, and who needed it? He wanted desperately to love and be adored in return; the problem was, where to start? Aleister reckoned the glorious day was fast approaching when he would subscribe to a competitively priced Filipina marriage agency: a flourishing Oriental avenue of commercial intimacy open to post-prime Occidental bachelors, widowers, and/or divorcés. Perhaps it was one instance where those innumerable, inscrutable Chinese have erred? Granted, tiddlywinks constitute rising stars within our rough, tough species: fitted to survive amongst strangers as segregated immigrants, or, thanks to Beijing's mushrooming economic leverage, to lead a global mercantile system; but in eugenic terms, they're junk people. Spawned from a passé imperial culture, informed by screeds of dynastic court archives, traditionally square-looking and businesslike. Not at all to Aleister's flighty, eclectic taste, the sources of which remained a mystery.

Aleister supposed that his sartorial bent toward *la dépêche mode* was rooted in the days of Pearly Spencer and tragic second-order observations made while orbiting creation on his own lonely planet. During year three, Pearly earmarked his old lady on one of her excursions to Brent Cross shopping centre. A haunted, milky-white escapee from Northern Ireland's sectarian troubles, Pearly was employed as a liveried bouncer in Mothercare: incendiary eye-candy with access to the retail facility's inner sanctum. Giggling, they'd disappeared through a doorway signposted 'staff only' and fornicated behind a clutch of industrial wheelie bins positioned in a designated waste storage area at the end of a poorly lit service corridor. Abandoned, snivelling wee Aleister was left to traipse unsupervised around the well-stocked mall, pressing against the glass exteriors of interchangeable shops, mixed-brand department stores, fashionable clothing boutiques, electrical retailers, on-trend accessory vendors, or luxury goods emporiums hosting award-winning Provençal face cream concessions. Whatever. Aleister stared inside like a piqued Martian. Exhilarated by the non-stop abundant varieties of fast-moving consumer goods, but deflated by consumerism's inconsequentiality, Aleister grew up to conceptualise existence as a shaggy dog story. Defiantly, he recollected window-shopping as a fond childhood memory. His mother's carnality, not so much, or her wuthering post-coital gawp from hooded eyes that neither knew nor cared about the developmental damage being done. In time, trips to Hendon's materialistic funfair petered out: perpetually liquored up, Pearly lost his clip-on neck tie, his job and his studio on Childs Hill. Aleister's mother's girlish infatuation withered as Pearly metamorphosed into an impotent homeless mendicant lumbered with untreatable cirrhosis and sleeping with rats in shop entrances down Kilburn High Road.

Looking up, Aleister was struck by dyspepsia, and another blast from the past. Across the pedestrianisation stood Immanuel Klein, a player who purported to abhor all things ci-devant. He hadn't changed: a buzz fed through the grapevine asserted that he was still a cunt. Aleister and Manny had met as high schoolboys selling imported designer schmutter across local trading Lanes (Leather and Petticoat), working for Lillian Skry & Ronnie 'The Knocker' Zucker, whose Uncle Joe Arzi's influence reigned supreme over Camden and Tower Hamlets' licencing systems, controlling market inspectors and subletting stalls. Manny fell in love with couture stock, and in due course became a right fashion victim, philosophising on the topic with all the brio of an art-house radical (a radical wanker naturally). During his late teens, he'd formed Futurist Punx, a heavy rocking four-piece combo that extolled beauty in strife. They jumped into bed with the louring Brigadier Robert d'Alby, a scary ex-forces cove turned small-time impresario for fledgling voices panegyr-ising insubordination. A genuine brute, the cigar-smoking brigadier was pretty mixed up; possessed of archetypal officer baggage, viz: horse-haired duelling scars, pent-up aggression, institutionalised homophobia and a mindless desire to assault anyone, or anything deemed officially dishonourable on be-half of manly ideals. Manny insisted the end justified macho means, opining that d'Alby's intriguing personality compelled exertion. It couldn't last. An accomplished cubist, BR'd and his easels disappeared one day, never to return. Without the insensate brigadier at the tiller, Manny's ensemble petered out. Aleister recollected a few trite lines from their one and only seven-inch: *Post-Minimalist Self-Portrait*: 'We shall sing of the thrill of danger/Flying fist-fuck up the arse/Courage, movement, hard rebellion/Sniffing glue in Regent's Park.' It was pompous tosh really. Thank you!

The brig booked Futurist Punx on a tragic tour of shite gigs at workman's clubs spanning the London Boroughs of Cam-den, Westminster and Brent. They were awkwardly on the bill alongside traditional Irish balladeers: Dubliners tribute bands for the most part. Manny boasted that he and his conjoint collaborateurs were waking punters from feverish hypersomnia; he glorified cruelty, thuggery, seven drunken nights, and wild injustice, but shat himself and ran for his life after being glassed while exiting the ladies' in Cricklewood Production Village. After that moment of self-discovery Manny gave up being a front man, and segued back into the supporting cast of his family's extensive business interests. As part of a tribal initiation ceremony, Manny swore to fraternise no more with associates hailing from families or enterprises unrelated to and/or unaffiliated with the Klein's expanding empire for one lunar year.

Manny kept his promise for the most part, only lapsing in a couple of lunations; firstly while tripping on brown blotters during a Hampstead Heath night-swimming weekend. Under the influence, he had confessed to Aleister that perceiving himself as an expendable, landless, fungible itinerant in a suicidally stratified society feverishly cannibalising greed, fear and malignant narcissism had brought him to his senses. He accepted he couldn't survive alone in Cuntish Town, that listless dive peopled by dawdling vagabonds. Aspirational London's galaxy of burnt-out wannabees, where genuine pretending passes as an adequate mode of existence, and lowbrow participants are deceptively orchestrated on behalf of ruling elites (for the sorry sake of fading public-minded perceptions) by arch-facilitators, activating media-managed biases to foment prejudicial ego-dystonic sensitivities. And so he'd pursued a safety-in-numbers logic, strategically allying himself through his bloodline to Albion's Premier Grand Masonic Lodge: an institution that aggregated supernu-merary groups of abominable opinion formers. As a party to which, his tribe pretended, under warrant, to present pragmatic balanced solutions to travails faced by ordinary folk tholing their humdrum lives. Adding in peroration, that he'd lost all his honest, salt-of-the-earth mates; but out of necessity, he'd changed. Manny petitioned for righteous understanding and forgiveness; appeals that were rejected by Aleister, who couldn't, and wouldn't confer his imprimatur. Nowadays, made-man Manny weltered amidst an orgy of sensual gratification, surrounded by heavies togged up in black leather, rubber and shiny PVC. They were his disciples, hook, line and sinker. Body harnesses, panic snaps and meat tenderisers eradicated any notion of revolt. Their overseer, whom Manny jocularly dubbed Jack the Rimmer, a hefty mouth-breathing automaton, was responsive to his masters needs alone. Kept firmly in check by a remote-controlled erection trainer, and subdued by double-bar nipple clips, Jack's enjoinders were slurred due to a fetish for adjustable velvet tongue gags, but he dealt severely with backchat or obstinacy within the ranks: lashing out with his customised sauna whip, that, along with a latex executioner's mask, constituted his vestments of office and tools of domination.

Manny's extended family (a loud bunch of perfidious, po-faced, holier-than-thou, hypocritical wheeler-dealers) started as mozzle and brocha speculators who struck lucky. Establishing a London variety business during Soho's vaudeville era, they grafted to nourish a lucrative customer base, and thereby curry favour with potential backers, to whom they pitched investment opportunities via a network of transcultural channels. Backed to the hilt, during World War Two they were able to boast, like the Windmill Theatre, 'we never close'. Embroidered into the red-light districts' bohemian tradition as a cool metonym for emancipation, the Klein's (alongside cut-price facsimiles) were on hand to cash in as the swinging sixties dawned. When it did, the K-mob became synonymous with navigating censorship and regulation, as parliament tacitly sanctioned Soho's erotic cabaret boom: customers were obliged to pay fees and join clubs as members an hour before admission. Thereafter, mischievous neo-Rabelaisian entertainment was permitted under law. By enthusiastically promoting liberation, lies and ersatz rebellion from the tight closets of inhibition, pimping-up revue bars and befriending the repressed, Manny's family had won renown and favour. Alack, plebeian popularity doesn't pay utility bills; hence, the bottom line means being admired ain't worth bupkis. Not ones to rest on their laurels, the Klein's remained sharp enough to excise flagging old comrades: dropping en route the functional mantle they'd worn as pansexual rights activists. Conversely, having cornered London's hardcore porn cinema market, freedoms now required paying for; every customer was appreciated, no matter how rancorous. Or, as pontificated by Manny to Aleister (on his second relapse, just a few nights prior to his sacramental inauguration at West End Great Synagogue), over last-order beers in the French House: "...you see, collectively, we understand the technicalities of this world intimately. No one else has the beginnings of a clue. Without shame, we pretentiously relish explaining our expertly authorised view of what's unfolding as designed by our powerful clients, on whose behalf we issue whiny rejections whenever any dissenting voice speaks out. It's all smoke and mirrors, obvs. History's been knockabout fun up until now. If the truth be known, we're deployed as an integral module, part of our masters' ultimate authority toolkit, arranged to control public narratives, perpetuate obedience, keep society suppressed by dint of cultural supervision.' Once again, Aleister had been well over the eight, so the lion's share of Manny's self-promotional spiel went in one ear and out the other. Currently coming down around high noon (as per his custom on Freya's day), in preparation for a critical night out ahead, Aleister was practically sat upright on the wagon. Thusly, temporarily, conflicted clouds cleared, turbid illusion cleaved and, momentarily, lucidity was suffered to intromit with his feelings.

'Manny! I ain't seen you for ages, you old bender, how's it hanging?'

'Chambré to tepid, mon ami.'

'Tell me about it. I thought we were forecast to be basking under a hot sun regular now the ozone's been depleted.'

'Don't even go there. The climate's one thing about this city that will never change.'

'True. What's happening?'

'Man, I'm busy boyo. I've acquired all of Uncle Moses' clip joints, peep shows, pop-up massage parlours, along with his Swollen Gash™ topless kink kiosks—and I'm developing an avant-garde nightspot. We're naming it 'A Symphony of Expensive Contradictions'. It'll be the nuts.'

'Whoa! That's some itinerary.'

'Well its business feller, not casual soul-laundering. However, there are perquisites; for one, it keeps me engaged in absorbing hobbies: know what I mean? How about you, rude boy: still riding psychotheraputic hobbyhorses? Or are you solving trolley problems?'

'I weigh a person's worth not by financial assets but in their quotient of individuality, if that's what you ridicule. But no, my intermittent disposable income doesn't afford ongoing clinical indulgences, so I'm stuck with the difficulty of destiny over ease of narrative. Left to independently question and challenge, the unintellectual human condition homo sapiens sapiens blindly wallow in, sans patronage.'

'Splendide mendax on a shoestring; blimey, that's more of a rivka, than a brifka. Stand on me Ally Bally: it takes a real trouper to admit that they're miscast in life's revocable tragedy. I warned you already: there's no future in poverty; crying over unremittingly bleak situations without scope for cognitive entertainments.'

'There's a marathon of drudgery involved in signing-on for a pittance; however, I keep faith with Raimundo Pato, theatrical agent extraordinaire.'

'Charing Cross Ray's looking after you, is he? Well, good luck with that schnip! What are you doing in between working days?'

'Laxing dude: spending too much hard-earned money.'

'Splendid stuff; we must hook up- your shout of course.'

Immanuel K, with his costermongers' God complex, was no more than a wide boy: too reliant on the dark arts of vice, hype and spin to foster credibility; Aleister had no intention of flyting with him, so he allowed Manny's barbed comments to slide. They'd grown to loathe one another, but in the great scheme of things, this was a bagatelle. Both chaps smiled courteously. Their enforced separation had plainly contributed to stifle a candid conversation. Bored, Manny's morose minders shuffled; distrait, staring vaguely at some passing object, halted as if frozen; yet still, life's frenzied momentum raced through muscular, bondage-clobber-clad bodies, causing each tit weight to dangle nervously, like flies in a spider's web. 'Totally: it'll be a mercy mission, won't it? You're working too hard.'

'Better to live as a blazing meteor than die old gracefully.' Manny replied, adding with a smirk, 'It's a distraction, innit? The divine, as manifested within the universe, is my guiding light.'

'But mate, apart from cavorting with toy-boys, to what purpose? Or don't you care?'

'I'm occupying my atoms so intensely they'll refuse to leave me. Life's one big party dude, and that's purpose enough for me.'

'Yeah, right cock, but like, what's the end product?'

Through bored amber eyes, distrustful, assessing, imperious, Immanuel fixed a vulturine gaze on his dishevelled interlocutor. 'Does God's vengeance end? I think not, brother. Historical consciousness keeps mutating: suck it up. Relinquish your neurotic orientation to sew loose hems. Trust me. Anyway, let's groove on, because it's time to move on.'

'Wicked. I've got places to go, people to meet; sayonara, Special K.'

What's that bustling atom malarkey all about? The impulse of an elementally active person to act is so strong that it stultifies them from acquiring knowledge for the sake of apprehension. Just how did Manny Klein intend to blaze brightly in his dotage? And whatever happened to grace, friendship, honour and serenity? Aleister was confused. Having acted intuitively all his life, he now found it nigh on impossible to think straight; psychological experiences steadily degenerated, visceral doubts multiplied. Much of this deterioration was a result of his disastrous addiction to adulterated angel dust. Although Aleister had once cherished continuity and cohesion, his life was now an ungovernable slide show of no fixed span. Maddeningly, he couldn't fathom who was operating the projector, or where to find an exit; some heartless tummler was evidently savouring a jape at his expense, and whomsoever it was, must pay.

At the comedy club, Aleister and Piggy (his anosmic dealer) chopped and snorted lines, shared a splash of toilet humour and did the Spanish fly deal before Pigman was called out to strut his stuff. Wired, Aleister parked up at the bar where he met (of all people) Mickey Fagan. The thin, delicate figure with close-cropped hair that had stood in the dock a year before was a changed man. Quietly confident, having bulked up in the prison gym, Mickey wore a ponytail tied with a blue ribbon, stonewashed 501s and a baggy white t-shirt bearing the slogan 'Frankie Says Relax'. On stage Piggy was first up (plying his Lorcán the Lovable Leprechaun shtick), but died horribly. Even Fagan, langered on Nelson Eddy's earned from a morning running around Seven Dials for production companies, intermittently screamed 'Cobblers!' By contrast, Aleister continued to feel awkward in the heaving venue; it burdened him with its fuggy claustrophobia, making him feel unusually aggressive. Worse still, the next act was some gauche twerp named Curious Cecil Gruff: a wretchedly conceited squirt, half concealing what appeared to be some type of magic lantern. The coy way Cecil postured bothered Aleister no end. Who did he think he was? Jack the fucking biscuit? These ultra-negative first impressions combined into a kind of supranatural sensorium, retained, or rather translated, by a wounded hunter-gatherer within, multigenerational memories and random imaginings. Sensing his spar's discomfort, Piggy ambled across, hoping to rub balsam over Aleister's storm-tossed forehead. Piggy respected Aleister's honest independence, but all the para-noid instability worried and depressed him.

'Whatchathink? The big time, or late night Channel Five?'

'Magic Pigsty: absurdly optimistic as always, buddy; don't give up your day job. How about this dodgy Cecil chap- you know him?'

'No; nor does anyone else. I bumped into him in the green room earlier. Curiously, he confessed to being a failed conceptual artist, but gruffly stressed he'd learned his lessons, and nowadays stands before us as the self-proclaimed king of multivalent comedy.'

'FFS Pigster, Equity shouldn't hand out union cards to the likes of Cecil. His sort touts angular collisions, rough ragged edges, raising voices of wrack and ruin. Amoral disorder oughtn't to be assimilated into the federation of performing arts. Cecil's idea of merrymaking is a monstrous anomaly, and best omitted. Look, I know this sounds Radio Rental, but I've witnessed Cecil's repertory of treachery erenow, in my previous Mesopotamian existence, around the time a great famine gripped the people of Babylon, and settlers from Uruk conspired with Šamaš-šuma-uk to plot evil.'

Enough! Piggy's clients were prone to puerile enunciations, so he remained silent, sipping maraschino via ruby lips; just about every situation is sanable. As far as Pigsty was concerned, each chap's concept of subconsciousness was an extraordinary piece of storytelling, trying to present ways in which structural systems have explanatory force- simultaneously unknown, yet effectively present. The key question remained: what the dickens did Cecil represent to Aleister? Piggy gave him a gentle tweak on his inside leg, and smiled. Piggy was a flirt, a proper card, a doughty lemon squeezer. Aleister was glad of Piggy's playful company; it steadied him. Equanimity calmed Aleister, fending off eternal verities tampering with his mneme; turning around to admire Piggy's glabrous countenance, possessed of soigné parity to Parian marble , he responded: 'Your round, innit, geez?'

It was tough improvisational shit he'd sold to Aleister; it was shamanic, coming on strong. Even flea-ridden mongrels like him weren't guaranteed to handle deep funk action like that. Piggy peered into Aleister's mince pies for reassurance. The bitch seemed cool. Joyfully, Pigsty drifted away: a trackless spore in a hot, humid dusk. Meanwhile, Cecil continued to push his luck, displaying a barbaric propinquity toward taking the piss. Using grotty rhetoric, the pawky manner in which he mockingly depicted community values threw a shitty spanner into the central mechanism of society's psychical economy; devaluing core theories at the very heart of its exchange rate. Self-proclaimed Royalty: do me a favour! Cecil was simply out for what he could lay his grubby paws on.

He couldn't give a tuppeny-toss about all the fools deluded enough to idolise him. In bygone days, human behaviour had mirrored unimpeachable elders; folk trusted digestible rules and felt safe under the protection of pedagogical politicians hoving flinty principles, like Saint Thomas More, or James Keir Hardie: gentlemen of integrity, sinew and fibre who stood or fell on ancient fundamentals. *Ab immemorabili*, more martial, but equally legendary, leaders flourished: Thor and Odin, brass-balled and hairy, who led from the front; demigods eager to share even their dying energies with a beloved natural environment. From those vanished golden-ages onwards, subsequent hero-less governments had been as corrupt as Narnia in winter. Aleister's revelatory thinking swayed toward regicide, because organically (apart from that soggy-knickered Granny-shagging stuff) Fagan was spot on: any demagogue, quasi-prophet, or tin-pot opportunist seeking to subordinate our painstakingly patchworked communities had to be dissuaded in the most brutal fashion, lest we poor people suffer. To be ill-governed under heavy manners is to be inspected, spied upon, directed, law-driven, regulated, preached at, controlled, censored, and/ or bummed by creatures that have neither the right, nor the wisdom, nor the virtue to do so.

For example, the Queen of England safeguarded sovereignty for a cadet branch of the haunted house of Saxe-Coburg-Gotha: landed gentry poncing like bejewelled tapeworms off successive populations of the British Isles since 1840. Her Majesty possessed arbitrary powers of pleasure over star-struck subjects, and took the preposterous title of Supreme Governor on Earth of the Church of England.

How mad's that? Because structurally, amid the white-hot foundry of Christ's notional Kingdom, there is no private property, no operationally leased airspace above buildings, or on rooftops, capped with newfangled mobile phone ærials, no pride and precedence, no commercialised motives and no reward save love. Ah, love. Today, schoolchildren are groomed from the age of four, force-fed fairytales, stuffed full of ornamental gibberish, and unwise additions dreamed up by the unintelligently devout, concocting thereby a miasmic paraphrase of the lifecycle of a mysterious first-century Palestinian Jew: stuff and nonsense that kiddies must fit onto the same mental map as the lifecycle of a hungry caterpillar (to which it bears a striking resemblance). A diabolical cult of the individual surrounds Queen Elizabeth (whose face, as designed by Arnold Machin, appears on all legal currency and postage stamps); leeching it large in magnificent palaces with stunning gardens, she's become the richest witch in the world. What on God's green Earth does Fagan see in her? Her every public relations action, no matter how banal, is lauded by a crass, fawning, sycophantic media; dark forces choreograph accompanying, pro-royalist demon-strations. Lurking behind Blighty's stylised figurehead, a voracious clique of parasitic castrators rule a decerebrated majority who scribble the traditional mark of inutile illiteracy by one of three names twice a decade (although some unlucky blighters from outside the portcullis, beyond the motte-and-bailey, are procured by palace security chiefs for the dubious privilege of being humped by princes, whilst sky-high on drugs).

'And now you children of my father's flock, the stochastic moment arrives to realise the implicatures and insurmount-

able powers of conviction.' Cecil trumpeted forth mesmerising messages: '… there can be no life without injustice,
no living creature can live and thrive without destroying
another existing organism. Behavioural battles between one's
instinctual reflexes and conditioned roles brings painful
confusion upon one's soul! Please yourself people. Groove
as you feel, follow your nature, let's all remain real. Come!
Gather now; conceive infinity as it actually is.'

Slyly Cecil produced his spellbinding lantern (a theatrical
prop billed as a 'sovereign cognitive apparatus' over promo-
tional posters dotted around the West End) and proceeded
with a phantasmagorical exhibition of suggestive images: pro-
jections fraught with terrified mini-mammals, punctuated at
intervals by uglier scenes where he performed bestial deeds
on an array of plastic inflatables. This cynosure revealed
hedgehogs and multicoloured shrews pulling processional
carriages under the yoke of bipedal figures bearing antlers
or pointy protrusions akin to mountain goats. All manner
of inventive pictures were grotesquely distorted, conjuring up kaleidoscopic sequences of emotional and spiritual
depravity, eating into and becoming ever more pressing
upon the mindset of an audience agog. Tension grew, lewd
ladies cried out in ecstasy, for stark was Cecil's power. Gross
manifestations emanating from CCG's ingenious implement
of lurid exposure formed a veneered pictorial mimicry of
humanity, laced with vermin, smut, scatology, painting an
eerie irreligious triptych, echoing mediæval exemplars of

Judgment Day. Alternative cabaret disguised excavations into evils. Serving no teleological purpose, lionising deceit and betrayal, highlighting people's worst traits, Cecil triggered anxieties, disinterring a primordial adversarial fear of 'others'. FOMO spread across ranging horizons. Thatcher's atavism had won; employing rubrici branded: what's in it for me? His contemporaries were no longer willing to curb sensory whims and fancies. Shunning personal responsibility, compromise and sobriety en masse; wholeheartedly subscribing to brain-worms, sleight-of-hand and the cheap tricks Cecil used to corner TGI Friday's kippered meat market. Afternoon bled into evening; febrile scuffles broke out amongst rebarbative white niggers in the foyer, late arrivals, as incompetent as they were brutal: an irruption of non-thinking easily divisible boot boys, disaccustomed to harmonious mingling at an after-hours soirée. A transitive section of stage-struck punters crowding the auditorium were, by contrast, smitten by Cecil's spectacle to the point of sensualism. Aleister could feel a collective craving to edge closer to Cecil's enthralling contraption. Cecil had turned them on big time. He'd spit roasted the lot of them by talking dirty. Now they were ready to bend over and retake it where the sun didn't shine. Aleister guessed that promises of requited lust were scarce fodder for most heavily taxed, hard-working citizens, and now, thanks to Cecil's adept salesmanship, easy virtue had become an issue of the upmost primary significance. The gloating horny figure of Curious Cecil Gruff (who reminded him, jarringly, of his absentee father) pandered to illicit desires, playing upon biblical guilt and weakness by beseeching volunteers to feast upon the pabulum of his wicked craft.

Only a soupçon of sanity survived; it belonged to venerable Aleister, would-be guardian of an adamantine anus, thus not a man to die of ignorance.

Proper leaders, heterodox ones who care about citizens, set the correct tone. They regulate an equitable agenda- a so-called meritocracy- there's no inheritance, and the right people are elevated as a direct result of their worth to society from a pool of stakeholders, not just to-the-manor-born usurpers. Direct democracies draw people together: promoting mutual respect, forbearance, and shared faith; not knobbing domesticated animals, or abusing feeble folk in the way Cecil encouraged. His ghastly vision was no better than some dreadful divorced, single, or separated shag-fest where the winner took all in a cold, friendless, windswept coliseum of malice, mistrust and pædophilia. Deciphering the nuclear consequences of undiluted iniquities free-flowing through this pantomime's rudderless, ale-house intelligence, Aleister corroborated his heart for battle by swigging the dregs of his pint. Picking up Piggy's abandoned shillelagh , Aleister tried to get at CCG 'of the many gross improprieties', but was hindered in his quest by profane powers. The fluctuating phalange of punters, seduced into chaotic tumult, prevented Aleister from marching unto war. An obsequious horde serried together in anticipation of Cecile's grand slam finale: a human wave of pheromones, wafting sweat, semen, vaginal secretions, breast milk and urine; women bared their mammaries, whilst grown men chewed on leather belts and tapered cork butt-plugs. 'Seekers of saliva hear me well, and duly obey my command! Bend your knees in supplication to erotic plasticity, shaped and finely tuned by the true might of passion' yelled Cecil during his rhapsodical rodomontade '…now hold hands and circle me, oh relinquishers of the stoical void'.

Aleister wished to scream aloud in his eagerness to halt Cecil in his cloven tracks, yet was lost for words as an ominous shadow menacingly upstaged any notion of gaining attention. A teeny mælstrom of pastel hues appeared, pullulating into a racy nimbus over Cecil's brightly painted, carnival-style headdress, spraying out across the mosh pit like an expansive roman candle; showering mere mortals with star-spangled fairy cum. As the dust settled, an awesome three-dimensional monstrosity superimposed itself onto Cecil's spot on the thrust stage, endowing momentary invisibility upon tonight's barnstorming artiste: this gossamer Luciferian countenance, with an erect filamentous appendage sprouting from its brow, totally stole the show.

'What does he do for an encore? Shag minors!' Fagan's gravelly voice startled Aleister, and conveyed the impetus required to aim a well-deserved haymaker at Cecil. He struck his target so hard that Piggy's knotty walking stick snapped in twain. Before one could utter 'hocus-pocus', the garishly tinted bounder vanished in an acrid puff of smoke. Accusatively, a stranger demanded: 'What the fuck are you doing, you nutter?' Bunches of bug-eyed Muppets stared daggers at him; they may have purchased council houses, but none had the Aristotle to confront Aleister mano a mano. In panic they pointed at him with large foam fingers. Poltroon bastards the lot of them, yet their consensus was remorseless. Aleister just couldn't get a grip on what was occurring. He was so out of synch with the picture, it wasn't funny. Was he the guilty party? Is that why spars blanked him? Fagan had seemed contrite, and other acquaintances had given him short-shrift. Someone could've warned him if he was edging off the rails & out-of-fashion. Now, who would visit him in clink? The spotty Young Conservatives? Not a chance. Aleister could no longer handle this level of peer group rejection. At his feet lay CCG, at last bloody well mute; sprawled across the stage in fancy dress, shards of his Technicolor Woolworth's porch lantern scattered across the deck. A resident ship of fools was about to up anchor and mutiny, so he needed to scarper. He swivelled swiftly, nutted some character on the schnozzle, then was on his toes out into Leicester Square (the pungent stench of refuse contorted his expression); it was full of mad dogs with ticks, stretching muscles in his lower jaw as he roared back at them. He howled ripe obscenities, growling like a giant wolf from some Norse saga stuck in his head since the infants. His stature increased until all else appeared to shatter in his wake. As he raced through the green, hundreds of pigeons took flight in unison as if they were all tiny rockets; ICBMs, part of a first strike initiative aimed at destroying our planet. Blindly happy, in the depths of their ignorance, the population deserved mutually assured destruction: liars and cheats every last jack. Look! There's the Devil. Where? There. How do you know? Listen

my friend, the light from that bulb up there in the white as-
bestos Artex ceiling hit the Devil, and bounced off onto my
retina; quantities of microscopic sensory things miraculously
tingled in my mind. It was them telling my brain cells, no?
What? You're imagining things; you're rather gonzo, aren't
you? Am I bollox.

Sprinting through Coventry Street and beyond into Hay-
market, Aleister visualised that resistance was pure futility.
A Routemaster 12 fast approached, its number symbolising
cosmic order; he braced himself to sacrifice the prospect of
a virtuous life to the mirage of a high-minded death. The
omnibus hit him so hard it felt as if a fireball had exploded
inside his hairless chest; a massive bout of hæmoptysis started
to fill the airways of both lungs, energy dissipated from his
being, his peripheral vision occluded; other senses seemed
to operate autonomously. As he slowly drowned in his own
blood, up above, Fagan's drunken face leered down.

'Life ain't fair Aleister, not for you or me leastways. Sadly,
the likes of us see, across this big bad globe, we're suffered
solely to be exploited. Even my mate Trestle-Table was fucked
over. The filth dropped him like a hot potato when they
discovered he was bent. Truth is, he was disposable see? His
corruptible tendencies had gone undetected during routine
security screenings, then, right on cue, the OB terminated
his career: after twenty-nine frigging years! Oh well, every
guttersnipe knows that manmade hierarchies are about
princes and whipping boys, winners and losers, punishments

or rewards. Still, you done good son. You realised we can't let insolent twats like Cecil Gruff take liberties. I'd have done the same, only you beat me to it. Those yuppie wankers lapped it up like powdered pussies, as if Cecil was the greyhound's undercarriage or some kind of fucking Sumerian deity. And the English working classes, this lost generation of uncivilised souls, socially engineered out of barbarism and direct into decadence, fought amongst themselves as usual. Fuck 'em. Still you got him; the means justify the ends okay. Now, stay calm mate, I've brought a tasty reward in recognition of your fortitude. Nothing styptic, I'm afraid.'

After chortling and wobbling a bit, Fagan gradually genuflected, holding tightly onto Aleister's hand. With due care and attention, he produced a small wet pink object from his torn hip pocket.

'Ere me now, I extracted Cecil's sesquipedalian tongue. I'd have tampered with his greasy orifice had the opportunity knocked, but you know, been there, done that.'

This tribute, delivered in a final act of innocent albeit demented compassion, soothed Aleister; as death engulfed him, his last selfless wish was that his lifetime on magna mater's terrestrial sphere mightn't have been spent entirely in vain. And if a repository for his immaterial soul had indeed been preordained, he hoped that his crushed body would at least, as a rite of passage, be reincorporated into the cycle of life as sustenance for stray dogs, urban badgers, jackals, foraging swine, if not fed to eagles, birds of the heavens or fishes in the sea. Regrettably, he feared his cadaver would be clinically dismembered. Selected organs would be legitimately employed by scientists involved in pathological research; others reaped purely for profit and sold abroad by Hippocritical practitioners trading corpus components. Boiled in water that had been saturated with herbs containing tannins, shrunken scrotums are worn as protective amulets by handmaidens of Hanbi as they go about their murky duties. Deconsecrating screaming infants, innocent babes in arms, wrenched from impoverished families; torturing impuissant souls dredged from the substratum of an intercontinental social pyramid to harvest adrenaline glands for adrenochrome, at the behest of an ancient and illuminated order of orgiastic priests. Here is wisdom.

Scanlon looked out languidly on the slicked water of Ponden Canal. Undergraduates sculled past late afternoon revellers on overhanging apartment balconies. Craft ale and socialism. Positive toxicity and Pimms. Another evening shift loomed

Brickwork | Robert Graham

Scanlon popped another Extra. Chemical dependency had robbed him of some physical and mental attributes, so this had become his crutch. Born from a long line of chemical ancestry, he bore the scars of their indulgence. Birthed with tiny arms and puny, brittle legs, he had made the best of his 'condition', remaining independent, useful and employable. A burden on society he would not be.

The Ponden Mill development, seeded in the early noughties, had morphed into a cephalopodic spread and now, thirty years later, engulfed Leeds' city centre. Part of the great levelling up drive to create a 'Northern Powerhouse', the city had become the relocation choice of an affluent southern populace who harboured no desire to integrate with the provincials. They held no respect for the history of the city; to them, the Leeds of Syd Hynes, Norman Hunter and The Three Johns didn't fit the metropolitan vision.

Like any invasion, the incomers imposed their culture, to the point where the natives rejected the city centre, preferring to scrape out an existence in the much neglected boroughs. This modern day Harrying of the North was widespread, a n extension of Thatcher's deindustrialisation. The cobblestones were gentrified and the benefactors wallowed in their hubris.

Scanlon looked out languidly on the slicked water of Ponden Canal. Undergraduates sculled past late afternoon revellers on overhanging apartment balconies. Craft ale and socialism. Positive toxicity and Pimms. Another evening shift loomed. As night building manager, he was the 'go-to man' for the occupants of Ponden Mill Lofts, which were by far the most desirable block of the whole development—scoured of grime and pigeon shit and plastered with fake northernness. He popped another Extra as he scanned his security pass at the entrance door. Chemicals helped him endure and primed his tolerance. He prepared himself for another twelve hours of servitude.

'Not much to do. No real issues except for corridor lighting on levels three and four being temperamental. I believe there's some kind of shindig on the top floor tonight so there will be some coming and going,' Ames reported.

Log handovers rarely contained anything to excite. The night shifts could be busy up to midnight with returning occupants and takeaway food deliveries but, all in all, the job was straightforward—if you could stomach the career-driven inhabitants and their impedimenta whom he was expected to doff his cap to.

'Av' you got anything for me? Ease my pain and such,' Ames asked. Like most suburbanites, he was a user.

'Only Extra. Not much else about. Can give you a couple

of these.' Scanlon held out two purple tabs.

'I owe you, man. Have a quiet one.' Ames hungrily pocketed the drugs and picked up his paper and coat.

'Oh, by the way: that creep on the top floor—you know, the retired surgeon—has two girls with him. They arrived about three. I haven't seen these ones before, but you'll notice them—spaced out schoolgirls. The fucking old perv. Thought he had a dodgy heart. Hope they see him off.' Ames winked and departed.

Scanlon tuned the office radio. Classical vibes were the order of early evening: Elgar would ease him into the evening chores. As night descended, 125 bpm would be the listening of choice. He dumped his rucksack and set out on his first round of the night.

His routine had taken five years to establish, and now he believed he could circumnavigate the building in the quickest and most efficient manner possible. First stop was the notice boards in the foyer. He would scan these for insights into the everyday psyche of the fellowship of residents. Flyers for pisspoor bands in tarted up tap rooms, esoteric art exhibitions for the pompous and talks by college dorm lefties, framed by taxi numbers, fast food menus and house regs. Pretentiously concocted art pieces adorned the foyer, some created by the residents, and mock graffiti plastered the tiled wall panels. The marriage of cherry-picked street culture and middle-class sentiment didn't sit well with Scanlon.

The rest of the building was much the same: corridors illuminated by motion-sensitive LEDs, two central lifts and east and west staircases. All manageable for a freak with flippers for arms and matchsticks for legs. The corridors were claustrophobic—obviously, the developers had made the decision to sacrifice communal space for larger apartments. No noise escaped said apartments—soundproofing and insulation had been a priority in the design. The only natural light that entered each floor was through the large windows on the staircase landing. Scanlon would often stop on his rounds and scan the city from one of these. A city-within-a-city now existed: a corpulent, bloated centre surrounded by anæmic, deoxygenated suburbia.

On the third floor, two giggling, whizzed up schoolgirls approached. 'It's Albie,' they screeched. Scanlon knew them as Beth and Chloe: Monkswood girls whom he often bought a bit of gear off.

'You finished today?'

'Easy peasy, lemon squeezy, Albie. The old fucker only wanted a bit of a lezzie show and a handjob. We done him in tandem.'

'You got anything other than Extra?'

'Well darling …' Beth wrapped herself around him whilst Chloe rummaged in her shoulder bag. 'Imbibe the contents of one of these little packages, Albie darling, and you are on the next rocket to Russia,' Beth whispered in his ear.

'You two are fucking angels in disguise. What do I owe you?'

'Not cheap, Albie, but fucking worth it. We'll catch you next week; old fucker wants a repeat performance.'

The two skipped off down the corridor. Scanlon decided he would stick to Extra tonight and keep his latest acquisitions for special.

The tab he'd dropped prior to starting the shift was starting to kick in as he finished his survey of the fourth floor. Good timing, he thought, as he unlocked the exit door to the roof space

Was it Extra or atavism that gave him his perceptive clarity? As far as he knew, he was the only one that could see the children. They came out of the brickwork, out of the beams, from under the plaster. Every shift, they would wait for him in the attic. There were seven of them, ranging in age from infants to young teens, all afflicted by their past, their stunted childhoods ingrained in the fabric of the building.

Small, agile bodies had enabled them to scavenge under looms. Nimble digits had tied snapped threads. Working up to sixteen hours a day, they had been broken before they were out of their early teens.

Three played hopscotch on a roughly marked-out grid, one perched high up on a crossbeam, the other two sat with Grace. Grace was the mother hen. George, blinded at the age of eight, was always on her knee and Elspeth clung to the comfort of her apron. All the children were dressed in the uniform of the mill—grimy gowns, raggy smocks, threadbare trousers. Half starved, pallid and dirty, they'd lived out their short, abused lives enslaved to the mill.

'Look who's come to play.' Grace announced Scanlon's presence and the children gathered around him.

'We want to go to the party,' the children implored.

'After all, only you can see us,' Grace reassured Scanlon. 'This is our playground, not theirs,' she petitioned her gathered brood.

Extra accentuated the scene before him. The children were so organic and alive. Their smell of lanolin and earthiness was a heady compound. The intoxication was stratospheric. Scanlon backed away to the door; the giggling brood surrounded him,

'WE WANT OUR FUCKIN' MILL BACK!' Grace screeched as he made egress from the scene.

The aged beams and the bare brickwork of the Victorian structure raced at him as he descended to the office. Head pounding, blood rushing, he collapsed into his swivel chair. In an attempt to steady his nerves he reached for the bottle of Glenlivet buried in the bottom drawer of the office desk. Drinking on the job was a sackable offence, but as long as forbearance was exercised, it was tolerated by the management group. Sitting back, feet up, a good draw on the bottle burning its way into his gut, Scanlon observed the scrawl made by small, greasy digits on the office ceiling—crudely formed letters, a mixture of capital and small characters but clear in their intent, 'oUR PlaYHOUSE'.

Scanlon felt that he and the children shared a mutual empathy, born from their industrial disfigurement and his Thalidomide condition, binding them to their common end—ridding the mill of the incomers.

Scanlon opened the service doors to Deliveroo vendors.

'Delivery for the top floor, number six; must be some party going on tonight.' The foreman ushered two underlings forward with thermally insulated bags of food.

'Fuck me: 320-quid's worth.' Scanlon checked the delivery order and signed for it.

'Talk about feeding cherries to pigs.' The foreman separated the delivery receipt and handed Scanlon the copy.

Banh xeo pancakes, pho soup, cau lau noodles, mandu

dumplings, crispy seaweed, sticky chicken and kimchi—the best east Asian cuisine that Leeds could offer. Scanlon surveyed the delivery note—a small fortune spent on noodles and dumplings whilst on the estates, bellies ached.

'Time for the special stuff.'

Scanlon opened the thermal bag and laced the food with a couple of grams of Rocket to Russia. Bag resealed, apartment six informed, Scanlon took the rest of the powder himself. No kick, but experience had taught him that slow burners were always the biggest hit.

It wasn't long before he heard Mouth Almighty approaching, talking like a tape in rewind, rehashing his daily intake of beer-glass liberalism. It stuck its red, bloated fizog around the office door. 'Food for number six,' he said, pointing at the bag.

'Yep, all yours.' Scanlon eyed the bespectacled female sponge that accompanied the mouth. Himalayan linen and a t-shirt emblazoned with 'eLECTRONICA.' She offered an insipid smile to Scanlon.

'Call in later, have a snifter, chew the fat.' The mouth was definitely out to impress the sponge with his cool.

'Will do.' This was one shindig Scanlon couldn't miss.

Over the next hour or two, party guests arrived. The demographics of the group served up no surprises: childless sycophants, au fait flakes caught up in their own versions of themselves. These ambassadors for the New North, bearing gifts from the boutique delis and wineries of Kirkgate, wore blandness like a uniform. Scanlon opened the door for them, let them in and sealed their fate.

Scanlon, now surfing on the special stuff, sensed a shift in the mill's being. He was now inside a living, self-regulating organism. The corridor walls were ringed by musculature supplied by a rich vascular system and the floors were a turbulent stream. Synapses fired. Static crackled. The structure's arteries pulsed with a peristalsis that sucked him towards the top floor. This was all so vivid, so real. The mill was shifting its equilibrium to deal with the engulfing viral gentrifiers; its immune system was primed, and Scanlon and the children were its platelets and corpuscles.

The door to number six was open. Syd Barrett's ditty about a cat called Lucifer Sam beckoned Scanlon to enter. Twenty-odd guests, corduroy and second-hand chic, bewitched by the special stuff. Eyes wide open. Grace was holding court.

Mouth Almighty's head had taken on the look of a fat, flaky sun-dried tomato. He was ready to pop. Elspeth and Annie had adopted him as their maypole. Teasing his unfettered ponytail with their tiny fingers, they placed a plastic bag over his head and held it tight. He was too fucked to resist. Two of the children had guided a line of guests out onto the balcony. The smallest child, Harold, tiptoed along the handrail; members of the line were being encouraged to follow and fall.

Grace urged the children to embrace their freedom and express themselves in carnage. The mill walls throbbed, revelling in the fightback.

The sponge danced to Phædra whilst children splattered her with kimchi and spicy noodles. Grace, from her perch on the open-plan kitchen island, sprayed lighter fuel over the main shelved wall. Prog rock and Prokofiev were transformed into a powder keg.

Scanlon's jellified legs wobbled and deformed. Absorbing all around him he collapsed to the floor. His fall was cushioned by a bug eyed Frank Sidebottom. The oversized cartoon head looked at Scanlon and said in a nasal, helium-tuned drawl ,

'I couldn't find a better example of the Stockholm syndrome. All these fuckers are endeared to the children yet they are being led to their demise.' Scanlon stared into the camped up social scientist's permanently frozen half smile and broke into a paroxysm of laughter.

Out on the balcony, guests continued to walk the plank. Harold covered his giggles with his fingerless right hand as he guided them to their demise. Grace clapped and ushered him back to her side. She gave him the lighter fluid. He knew what to do. He doused the food-splattered sponge with the flammable material. Grace, with Georgie on her knee, reached into her apron pocket and handed Scanlon a box of Bee's Knees matches.

'The Thalidomide kid strikes a blow,' Sidebottom, acting as MC, announced to those guests left standing.

Scanlon took a match between his teeth and scraped the phosphorus head along the box edge. He spat the lighted match onto the solvent-soaked bookshelf. Ignition was instant. Scanlon retreated from the intensity of the heat and took up a position by the full-length sliding windows. The sponge combusted seconds later, whirling like a fiery dervish, much to the delight of the children, who danced around her holding hands. The Frank Sidebottom lookalike struggled to remove his melting polystyrene head. Death by caricature was imminent.

Grace cradled Georgie in one arm. 'Come, naughty boys and girls, the party's over.' Blackened, charred infants trooped out of the apartment and danced under the corridor sprinklers. Grace turned to Scanlon. 'You'll be joining us soon.'

Through the shrillness of the fire alarm, Scanlon could hear 125 bpm. A rave had kicked off on the square below. Locals from the estates were flocking into the city, reclaiming the streets, celebrating a renaissance. Flames erupted from the high-rise panorama like beacons ignited to spread the message across the North. Scanlon climbed onto the balcony rails, surveyed the anarchic scenes below and bellowed, 'THE NORTH WILL RISE AGAIN!'

At the Bay Horse that night he was complimented on his professionalism. He was an ice-cold killer, according to his client, and the regulars took to calling him, with a mixture of derision and respect, Deadly Dougan

Victims | David Rogers

By the time he hit forty-five, Derek had spent two decades working night security in factories, warehouses, building sites and industrial estates.

He avoided commercial contracts if he could because they wanted him on his feet all night and they had key systems to check he was. Industrial estates were the best. On those, he could stay in his control centre for practically the whole of his shift. All he needed to be happy was an electric heater, a kettle for his Nescafé and a microwave to warm the chip-shop pies he bought from Harry's on his way in (the first job of the evening was to throw away the sandwich his wife had made—the default was a doorstep slathered with margarine and processed cheese).

The best jobs were on big building sites, because there was usually a canteen, and that meant the special pleasure of a breakfast supper in the company of men whose day was just beginning. And the food was superb. Fried bread, crisped to golden perfection. The bizarre-when-you-think-about-it combination of fungus and foetus, cooked until the former became dark and flaccid and the latter developed a rubbery resilience. Discs of black pudding burnt to scabs. The only doubtful element were the tomatoes, which resembled something left in a kidney dish after a post-mortem; the best was the bacon, which had soaked in fat until it acquired a texture like melting velvet. Whatever. He loaded it all onto his plate and helped it on its way with a mug from the urn and a lengthy contemplation of the half-naked 19 year old in that morning's *Star*.

In his later life, when he thought back to those days, it was always winter when he left the site. Morning twilight, streaks of yellow through a chain link fence. Pale brown puddles in the car park crackling under his boots, the welcoming smile, the supple body, of Kirsten from Daventry glowing in his mind like the B&H he lit in the wind's first gap.

When he got back he took his wife a cuppa and undressed in the submarine light of their bedroom. He remembered condensation puddled on the window sill, everything slightly damp. Intimate, sour smells from under the duvet; soft, stubbled flesh; sweaty creases; perfunctory sex on the rare occasions she was receptive, then falling asleep to *Five Live!* while she heated the milk for Nancy's Weetabix.

He was on the gate of the Townsend Industrial Estate the night after a big delivery of copper wire came in. There were twenty two-metre-diameter bobbins stacked in the yard: four columns of them, each higher than the perimeter wall. Colin made a special journey over from Luton to brief him on it.

'I'll tell you what,' he said, 'that copper's worth a lot of brass, so it'll be a magnet for the fucking pikeys, Derek. Mr Kovacevic said they won't get it into the ground for a week at least, so both eyes peeled, yeah?'

They came that same night. A silver transit parked on Westbury Close. Two of them wandered up to the sealed window and rapped on it with something metal. He waved at them to wait and picked up the phone to call in an alert. They rapped faster and shouted when they saw this, but he switched off the external mic and finished his report. He was told to sit tight and they'd get mobile over in five, ten at the latest.

He put the phone down, walked over to the window and held out a hand with the fingers extended. That stopped the commotion, and one of them walked back to the van. The other stayed and tried to say something in a normal speaking voice. He was young, with long blonde hair and ginger sideburns.

Derek walked back to his desk and switched the microphone back on.

'You didn't have to do that, you know, chief.'

He ambled back to the window.

'Can I help you, sir?'

'Look at you. Man doing a dog's job. Must be a lonely business, though, stuck out here all by yourself. *Are* you lonely?'

'If there's nothing you want, sir, I'll have to ask you to leave the premises.'

'I do want something. I want to know if you ever get lonely. Can't be good for the old mental health, eh?'

'Well since you ask, sir, I'm not lonely. Not at all. I have lots of friends and they're just a phone call away.'

The man gave him a lop-sided grin; Derek kept his face rigid.

'Alright, chief. You have a good night, now.'

The next day Colin was once again waiting for him. He'd done some checking. Dry bright was going for £3,600 a ton at Remarkit, so there was something not unadjacent to £25,000 sitting on the concrete back there.

'It's the Chinkies,' he said. 'They buy it all up. Copper like that these days, it's worth its weight in gold.'

For a moment Derek thought he was going to offer to sit in with him, but that wasn't Colin's style. He wouldn't undermine an employee by implying he couldn't cope with a challenge. Also, he was a lazy cunt.

Jobs like that, where you just watched screens all night and did three or four walkabouts, the real challenge was finding ways to kill time. Derek usually put on Heart FM and read something from the carrier bag of paperbacks he picked up in Bedford market once a month. There was a stall in Harpur Square that sold them by the kilo. He could just about get through one in a shift, if there were no distractions.

This night it was Harlan Coban's *No Second Chance*, but he couldn't concentrate. It was like when he did his GCSEs.

He felt tense and trapped, and he wanted to … to do some-thing. To be somewhere else. In the end, he lowered the book and started watching the four-by-three-grid of CCTV screens as though they were showing actual programmes.

Just before midnight he thought he saw the silver transit go by on the outside feed, but if that's what it was, it carried on up the Townsend Farm Road.

Then, about 20 minutes later, he saw her.

It was just for a moment—a thin figure in a black hoodie and a skirt, walking between C2 and C3. He watched D1 but she didn't appear. Nothing on B3, either. The buildings formed a rectilinear figure nine, with the security office at the gap between the upturned tail and the loop. If she was on C, she couldn't get out without going through the main gate.

He picked up the phone and held it in his hand, as if for reassurance, then he put it down again. He went to the window and peered out. Nothing. It was coming on to rain. He looked at the externals: just the odd car on the farm road, headlights flaring in the night lens. Mobile would turn up at three and he could mention it then. He knew what they would say. You know what your problem is, Del? You sit here six days a week wanking away the hours of darkness. Can't be good for the old eyesight, can it?

Finally, he put on his anorak and baseball cap and went outside. The security lights made sharp shadows from the edges of the tin sheds, the rectangular brick offices. The spools were where they were supposed to be. He walked up to them, past Houghton Regis Dental Supplies, Greenstar Mouldings.

She was standing in the doorway of Tulip Telecoms. He

approached her without saying anything. She looked at the ground and shivered, her hands in the pockets of her fleece. Her face was thick with cosmetics. When he put his arm around her, it was a shock. He could feel every rib in her chest, every knuckle in her spine. The dress she wore had been a black sateen ball gown. It had probably been made for a child; now it ended at mid-thigh, the hem frayed into threads. She unzipped her fleece, dropped it on the tarmac. He kissed her scabbed arms, her hands with their dirty fingernails, her stick legs, her feet. Her hair was ash blonde, surrounded by a halo of sparks in the sodium floods. It had a coppery gleam in the office's desk lamp. He never saw her pubic hair. She had no breasts. His hands were shaking, he remembered that. He fucked her against the filing cabinet, on his desk, on the floor. Her nose was wet, he remembered that, too, and the way she whimpered the whole time he was inside her.

When he woke up, he was parked beside a burger van on a truckers' lay-by on the other side of Milton Keynes. He sat in his car and watched between wiper beats as a man in chef's whites opened up and started work. It had gone ten before he returned home. The police cars were already in his drive.

Four years later, Derek received a phone call from a solicitor in Grantham. He introduced himself as Peter Davies and went on to say he was acting as the executor of his father's will. He was calling to inquire whether Derek and his brother wanted to go through the details before he put it in for probate. From the way he talked, it was clear he assumed Derek knew about the death.

Derek wasn't doing anything at the time so he applied to the authorities for compassionate leave and drove up one night in the late spring. He hadn't spoken to his father for ten years or more, so Davies had to talk him through what was what. The principal asset was the pig farm his father had bought after he left the RAF.

'Don't worry. There're no actual pigs there,' Davies said with a smile. 'Mr Dougan was in poor health for some time. He sold the stock and paid off the mortgage, so it's up to you whether you divest or restart the business. Either way, we'd be happy to act for you.'

The will assigned joint ownership of the farm to Derek and his brother Dan, who was living in Canada with his second wife. When Derek phoned to give him the news, Dan said he wanted the farm sold and his half of what it fetched paid into his UK savings account. Derek guessed he wasn't working over there in Vancouver, but neither was he back here in Dunstable. His GP had put him on Citalopram and he found it difficult to concentrate.

The house stood on one edge of a concrete yard; opposite it was a barn that held an ancient tractor and muckspreader. One side between was taken up with a byre, the other led to what had been the main piggery. The byre had a whitewashed tool wall holding syringes, forceps, shears and a double-barrel shotgun. Plastic sacks of Sharpe's pig nuts formed an island in the centre, and there was a cupboard filled with bottles of antibiotics and hormones. The piggery was made up of sheds with tar-paper walls and corrugated iron rooves. They were filled with breezeblock pens and farrowing crates.

The solicitor had told him that the probate process would probably take at least six months, so Derek drove down to the halfway house and got permission from the probation service to change his address. It was early June when he moved in to his ancestral home.

The summer came and ripened. Derek knew there were things he should be doing—finding an agent to carry out the valuation, for example—but he couldn't seem to make himself do them. Instead he put the television on all day every day, and stared at the curls of smoke from his cigarette, the steam from his coffee. Occasionally he went out for a walk. He saw purple foxgloves and cow parsley, heard the steady thrum of the A1. Once every three days or so, the phone rang, but he never answered it. In the evenings he felt a Pavlovian urge to go out, and although he'd never been much of a boozer, he got into the habit of driving to the Bay Horse in Swayfield for a few pints.

The same faces were in there night after night, a blokey embargo hampering everyone else's access to the bar. Strangers had to order their drinks from behind the line. They were handed over by one of the faces, usually with a quip for any women present.

At first Derek sat on his own with a Dick Francis, but little by little he was noticed, nodded at, and then drawn into their gang. He never said much, but that was okay. They liked his dullness, his lack of retaliation. They liked to have a larger audience for their outrageous opinions, the shouty politics that passed for conversation among them.

The leader of the group was a man called Garvey, who managed the Ladbrokes on Elmer Street. He followed Derek into the toilet one night and, talking while he pissed, told him about a little problem of his brother-in-law's. Go-Go Girl was the problem's name, and she was a four-year-old greyhound that had never been any sodding use and had cost the best part of three grand to buy, train, feed and race with nary a thruppenny bit in return. Now she'd done her hock and that was that—except that if she were kept at the trainers past retirement it would be £80 a month kennelling, a £200 deposit and who knows how long before she pegged out?

The brother-in-law turned up the following Saturday afternoon with Go-Go Girl in the back seat of his Subaru Impreza. He gave Derek the lead, refused a cup of tea and got back into his car to wait. Derek led the limping dog into one of the pens, took off its collar, quieted it down and killed it with his father's shotgun. The ears were tattooed with an identity code, so he cut them off with castrating shears and carried the lead and collar back to the brother-in-law, who gave him two £10 notes and drove off. Derek put on his dad's wellingtons and buried the dog in a midden behind the nearest sty.

At the Bay Horse that night he was complimented on his professionalism. He was an ice-cold killer, according to his client, and the regulars took to calling him, with a mixture of derision and respect, Deadly Dougan. The derision was because his victim had been a small, injured dog; the respect because most of them guessed they would've been a bit horrified by what was left after the shotgun discharged.

A week later there was a lock-in in honour of the landlord's wife's birthday, and plates of chicken drumsticks, quartered pork pies and cheese-and-Branston sandwiches were handed out. Towards the end of the evening, Garvey put his arm around Derek's shoulders and offered him a slim panatela.

'You know what, Deadly? I've been thinking about your situation, and I want to give you a little bit of financial advice. Now you've got about ten acres there and at the moment it's not bringing in a penny for you, is it? You've got to do something about that.'

Derek couldn't say different.

'You might rent it for pasture if you wanted a steady income. But have you thought about what you could make if you put your talent for canine euthanasia on a business footing?'

Garvey went on to explain that where they were, in the East Midlands, a gnat's pube from the A1, it was easy to get to a whole load of circuits. There was Nottingham, Peterborough, Birmingham, Wolverhampton, Sheffield, Pontefract, Bedford, Harlow … and those were just the places within an hour or so's drive. What he had to do was let the racing managers know he was offering a service, and they'd clue in the trainers. Maybe top it up with a few discreet classifieds in the *Greyhound Star*—post-retirement solutions, something like that. Garvey, who'd obviously put some thought into this, said he knew a few people who knew a few people, and if Derek wanted, he could help him get his enterprise off the ground. There was legal beagle over in Grantham who could draw up a little agreement, if he liked …

Derek's first capital investment in PR Solutions was a captive-bolt gun. At first there were no more than one or two dogs a week, but then word got around the circuit, and the customers came running.

They bounced out of their cars and vans with weightless tread. Some fawned on him, and when they did he rubbed the silky nap on their famished heads and led them to their pen. They complied. They were eager to please. They were wretched—the most naked animals on Earth, nothing but skin and bone, every rib visible. They shivered in the sunlight. They whimpered and pressed their embarrassed tails between their legs and licked the captive-bolt gun so that he had to lift it and reapply it to their foreheads several times before he could get the shot off. They were good at being victims. They died like dogs, thunderstruck.

Five blisters from the end of his last pack of Citalopram, Derek decided to go without for a bit, see what would happen. When nothing did, he felt a sense of dizziness and disorientation as the weight of the world lightened, and things came into focus around him. 'I feel like my old self,' he told the faces down the Horse—but really, he felt better than that. He was a new man.

For the first time in his life, he was interested in making real money. He felt sexual pressure again. He bought a computer, a coffee machine and a four-in-one Virgin Broadband package. He subscribed to the BBC Good Food website, and spent an afternoon making red onion marmalade. He answered the phone with the phrase 'PR Solution, how can I help you?' and when he heard Dan's voice he turned around and told him straight: dad's farm was staying in the family.

Derek's father had been something of an autodidact. Besides his horde of *Titbits* and *Sunday Express* colour supplements, there was a shelf full of editor's recommendations from the Heron Book Club. They had smudged print on 50-gram paper, PU leather bindings, and reflected the editor's rather conventional taste. In the evenings Derek read works he would never have considered before, such as *20,000 Leagues Under the Sea* (good), *The Trial* (bit weird, but also good), *Uncle Tom's Cabin* (toss), *The Compleat Angler* (first few pages only, kept falling asleep), *Paradise Lost* (had its moments), *Women in Love* (sounded promising, but toss), *Wuthering Heights* (toss) and *Pride and Prejudice* (total toss).

Meanwhile, out in the world, an ironic evening down the dogs was becoming a popular after-work option for the urban office worker, and greyhound syndicates were catching on across the country. As a result, national demand for PRSolutions' service grew like Topsy. After a while, the trainers started clubbing together and sending ten or more customers a time. Derek retired the bolt gun and laid a plywood sheet and a tarpaulin over one of the pens, then ran a hose into it from his car exhaust. At first he hired a mechanical digger and excavated a trench for the bodies, but later he just soaked them in red diesel and burned them.

'That's the thing, you see,' he told the faces down the Horse. 'That's the kind of productivity you get when the private sector is allowed to innovate.' They listened to him, too, and talked about him admiringly when he wasn't there.

Derek's only problem was the girl. She wasn't *really* a problem, of course, but at the same time she was, because she haunted him.

Night after night they met for the first time, and night after night he ran her over on rainswept roars, or dismembered her on zinc tables, or raped her in fairgrounds to the sound of a calliope organ and the smell of burnt sugar. One night she lay stabbed and bleeding on the lino of his stepmother's utility room, the next he was required, for reasons he was never told, to push her off the Clifton Suspension Bridge. And then the manhunt began. This was invariably led by officers from Bedfordshire police, assisted by a changing cast of former teachers, schoolmates, weathermen, DJs, his ex-wife and daughter, Colin, the occasional cabinet minister. Sometimes he woke wet-faced in the pre-dawn dark bent into a foetal clench, choking on reflux, only slowly becoming aware that none of it had really happened. Then he would spend the rest of the night reliving it anyway, after which, in his second sleep, it happened again.

As Derek's business blossomed, and his social standing rose, these dreams become milder and less frequent. Sometimes he and the girl did nothing more than bicker over a continental breakfast, or he was forced to wait while she tried on a pair of jeans in a department store. On the last night, she came transfigured into a beautiful, slender woman in a white silk wedding dress. They were in some kind of orangery, echoing to the detonation of champagne bottles—white painted iron, gardens through glass, mosaics underfoot—and she walked towards him with her arms open and her mouth smiling, shaking confetti from her gold hair, all the dogs alive again and foaming around her feet, licking his hands and face, every one of them a fucking cartoon—as though that was what redemption was: his more than hers, or theirs.

He bought Garvey out for a couple of grand and never looked back.

Ladies and gentlemen, please take your place in the heavenly realm! It's the old hierarchical layout and you instinctively know your position ...

The Electric Jesus Vagina | Steve Carter

Somewhere in the deepest level of Hell there is an infernal machine churning out positive affirmations, uplifting sentences, wise sayings and motivational outpourings. Serried ranks of demons then attach them to images rendered at 72-dots-per-inch, including, but not limited to:

Native Americans (very old, or young and hot)

Places of natural beauty

Laughing children

Lovers in the rain

Buddhist monks

Psychedelic art

Rainforests

Empty roads

Candles in darkness ...

On and on and on the list ripples out into infinity.

Thus Satan seeks to dissipate the sum of human wisdom. Complexity is reduced to sugary bite-sized morsels that appear tasty but never satisfy any real hunger.

The digital smörgåsbord is ever changing and ever the same as we nibble and regurgitate empty exclamations across the brightly coloured pixelated wastelands, enlightenment in twenty words or less, ephemeral momentary feel-good falsehoods that offer nothing beyond the initial mental rush and the self-congratulatory recognition of our reflections flickering on the surface of a shallow pool, mind numbing mantras drained of any real meaning.

Scroll on, brothers and sisters, scroll on. At least you'll get a dopamine hit as you grin inanely at the distorted patterns in your personal hall of mirrors …

Don't forget to click on the URL to visit the website for more trite mini-bites from the snake oil self-help gurus, quantum masters of the Art of the Spiritual Deal, whose hourly rates exclude the financially restricted (an unfortunate situation the poor have created for themselves through accumulated karma, or by not practising positive thought sufficiently to manifest a slice of the spiritual pie in the sky—some people just can't be helped …

Intense in delivery, self-consciously humble, carefully avoiding any real dialogue in favour of vapid profundities that crumble upon inspection, their target market not those who question.

Workshops to follow, complete with pay-per-view video streams, secret techniques to manifest your dreams, guided drug experiences to get you closer to your true nature, or commune with your soul, or meet the ascended masters, or the tribal elders, the Hindu deities, the alien watchers, the Earth Mother, the angels, the vegetal overmind. Take your pick …

184

The fortunate children of decaying empires seek the usual posthumous guarantee of everlasting bliss, sticky tar shadows ignored to stare into the light.

Guided by those more steeped in ritualised behaviour, muttering mantras or chanting in Sanskrit to a culturally appropriated projection of their own desire, as if some dead tongue would more likely attract the benevolent attentions of the higher realms. If that doesn't work, perhaps Latin might?

For the fortunate, all gods are there to be chosen between, measuring and evaluating to procure the most personally beneficial outcome. Those less fortunate generally stick to their local pantheon.

We are adoring Allah, beseeching Baby Jesus, bleating to Buddha, soliciting Shiva, prostrating to Pan, moaning at Mithra—hang on a second, ladies, I'm sure I've got one here for you somewhere … er … venerating Venus … go on, pick a deity—any name will do—reciting for rewards, grovelling for gifts, because we deserve it—we are the good guys, the white hats, the chosen ones, the devout, the sannyasin, beloved of the angels.

Aum mani fest me something nicer than this.

The gods for the most part remain silent. Or perhaps are just too busy elsewhere. After all, time is ticking, it's a big universe and in all likelihood, circling around some of the ten thousand billion stars out there, there are several million other planets supporting intelligent (careful with that word) lives that are equally persistent in their supplications to the divine, its image strangely shaped much like themselves, or their local flora and fauna.

But despite all evidence to the contrary never doubt that

your god is the right one, your special book is the repository of truth, your belief more valid than those obviously deluded others. There be dragons …

We polish our halos with the sweet wax of ego, getting ready to stake out our place at the big man's gathering of the great and good. Ladies and gentlemen, please take your place in the heavenly realm! It's the old hierarchical layout and you instinctively know your position …

On your knees.

Somewhere out on the periphery there is the sound of happy laughter and the leaden flap of leathery wings, barely audible over the saccharine drone of harps …

Also from Dog & Vile …

Elastic Waxes in Unbounded Media

A misguided fusing of meretricious Dionysian thuggery with crypto-Apollonian socio-illogical impenetralia. A phantasmagorical porridge adulterated by off-key goat songs, Lacanian membra disjecta and mechanically recovered existentialism. Buy and hate.
—Nadine Dorries

For as long as I can remember, ever since I was a wee bairn, I've wanted to be a deep-sea trawler. Many's the night I'd spend lying in bed, imagining myself ploughing white furrows over the black Iceland cod grounds, feeling the mighty engine vibrating in my belly, the thrust of the screw driving me onward against the thickening pull of the nets, the all-but-imperceptible tickle of the dungaree riders on my mighty back, my ice chest open in expectation of the glorious moment of up-haul and out-spill, when a thousands shining silver bodies would slide and wriggle across my plates and planks. Which was when I'd usually have to reach for a tissue or two … Sorry, what was the question again?
—'Demersal Dave' McIntyre

10 Unpublishable Fictions

It shows, if nothing else, the animating effect of mortality on the human imagination. Hysterical realism comes of age and gets a job marketing cycles of infection and death to the bike-riding public.
—Brigid Mahony

Can I ask why you sent it to us? There's literally nothing in here about the correct temperature of a terrarium.
—Frog Care Monthly

A doomed attempt to forcefeed art through the tightly clamped jaws of the general public.
—Frankie Dettori

I heard the first five purchasers would be offered a cheeky lagniappe—one night of ecstasy with the London Symphony Orchestra's woodwind section. No such luck, of course but, still … just *imagine* …
—Sir Roy Strong

Printed in Great Britain
by Amazon

33770720R00106